Ian Christon

DREAMS FROM COMMUNISM

SATIRE FROM THE PAST,
LESSONS FOR THE PRESENT

Copyright © Author Iantcho Hristov 2024

All rights reserved.

ISBN-13: 979-8-3461-7722-7

© Translation into English from the Bulgarian edition by Maria Samichkovska and Ivan Handjiev [2024]

Table of Contents

DISCLAIMER 1
KOMSOMOLSKA STREET 2
MAMA NEDA AND HER SON 20
THE GALABOVS FAMILY'S RIGHTNESS 36
WHO CREATES GOOD AND EVIL? 54
BECOMING A KOMSOMOLETS 70
THE PASSIONAL OF LITKO POPOV 89
TWO COMRADES 101
AN ILLNESS AND THEREAFTER 126
TWO CAPTAINS AND A CIVILIAN 138
PROFESSOR DRAGNI SHESTAKOV 154
PENYO THE DUCK 171
ONE STRANGE DOCTOR 184
ABOUT THE AUTHOR 199

DISCLAIMER

This is a work of fiction. Names, characters, events, and places within are either products of the author's imagination or are used fictitiously. Any resemblance to real persons, living or dead, actual events, or specific locations is purely coincidental. Some of the cities, villages, regions, localities, and resorts mentioned in these stories are fictional and bear no representation to any geographical place or map.

KOMSOMOLSKA STREET[1]

Komsomolska Street was a cross street of 9th Of September Boulevard[2] and was located in the heart of our small provincial town.

During the first years following the Red Army's invasion in Bulgaria and the "victory" of the September Revolution that followed it, the state underwent a frenzied transformation, heavily influenced by the Soviet model. A mass exodus from rural areas swelled the cities, where new housing projects sprang up – all sorts of residential projects, from single-family homes and mid-sized housing cooperatives to towering apartment blocks and dormitories. Everyone craved to have access to the amenities that those new homes provided. The entire state, so to speak, had already switched the railway tracks, changed direction, but the final destination was still out of sight, at least at that time.

---

[1] *Komsomol*: the youth division of the Communist Party in some of the countries in the former Eastern Bloc during the times of the Cold War. It was usual practice many streets to be named after various symbols of Communism.

[2] *September 9, 1944* is the date of the coup d'état that followed the invasion of the Red Army in Bulgaria and that became the turning political point which gave the start of radical reforms towards Soviet-style socialism, finally resulting in Bulgaria becoming part of the Eastern Bloc for the following 45 years, until 1989.

Following that pattern, Komsomolska Street rose quickly, lined on both sides with brand new apartment buildings built by housing cooperatives. Back then, the City Council used to seize the land for the new housing developments, while the rightful owners could choose an apartment in the new building which was about to be built on the same spot, or another one, somewhere nearby, or they were simply given some financial compensation. This land plot was then typically given to people with connections to the party, who would build cooperative housing buildings there, six to nine families in each. The apartments in these cooperatives were all identical, and the buildings themselves were practically twins: brick structures built on sturdy foundations, three or four stories tall, no elevator.

The construction of the cooperative at 3 Komsomolska Street followed a similar path, but with one key difference. Unlike its neighbors, this building housed the city's Communist Party leaders and the top brass of the People's Militia[3]. It boasted only three floors, yet each floor held two spacious apartments. These featured three bedrooms apiece, a living room, a separate dining room, and a bathroom with its own boiler. For its time, that building was the epitome of a perfect residence, and it proudly displayed a plaque on its entrance door reading "A Model Home", an honor bestowed by the Municipal Council on new cooperative housing properties of that level.

---

[3] That was the name of the Bulgarian police force at that time.

Work on the building had begun way back in 1965, but a lack of modern machinery meant the whole project dragged on for several years. While it was under construction, the future residents would often drop by to check out the unfinished cooperative and marvel at the floor plans. Annoyingly, some of them were demanding to change the interior layout, which caused extra headaches for the builders who were already struggling to meet deadlines.

The way the apartments in the cooperative housing on number 3 were awarded, once it was finally finished, was quite interesting. The system followed the hierarchical order of the time, with the high-ranking party officials getting right of first choice on the apartments. The second floor ones were the most hankered after, followed by those on the third floor, while the first floor apartments were the least attractive. One thing was clear to everyone in the city: the future inhabitants of this building would be all but ordinary ones.

Once the new owners moved in, time continued its relentless march and the years rolled by. Eventually, communism crumbled, and the country entered the course of democracy.

And so, forty years later, on a sunny day in September of 2008, an old, hunched man was sitting on the bench in front of the cooperative at 3 Komsomolska Street. The old man had rested his chin on his cane and watched the passersby thoughtfully. He wore massive shell glasses with thick lenses, which made his eyes look huge. He was dressed in a hand-knitted brown vest and cheap gray cotton pants.

Around noon, while the old man was still watching the passersby, an elderly woman in a faded yellowish dressing gown appeared on the terrace of the second floor and called out to him angrily:

'Ponko, it's lunchtime already! You've been hanging out down there all day! Do come upstairs already!' And without waiting for his reply, she turned and slammed the terrace door shut.

Ponko did not respond. He never did. He would go upstairs for a half-hour lunch, and then come right back down to sit on the bench in front of the apartment building, where undisturbed he would lose himself in his thoughts. People would walk past him on the sidewalk, and rarely did anyone greet him. Eighty years old, he had become a stranger to his fellow citizens. Forty years since the building went up, most of the original owners were gone, while their children and grandchildren had moved away – some to the capital, others to Europe or America.

Ponko used to spend hours on the bench in front of his home, often reminiscing. His thoughts were flitting through various topics in his head, but never lingering on any particular memory for too long. This was how he was spending his days throughout the summer and the autumn. Only the winters' cold kept him indoors for longer, but when spring returned, he would once again take up his regular watch on the bench.

Born in a village, years before the "victory" of communism, Ponko was a boy just like all the others. From quite an early age, he had started working in the fields and only scraped by in school until eighth grade. Truth be told, he hardly ever went to class. Sometimes he just had not enough time to spare, other times he just was not interested. Ultimately, he never really mastered any of the subjects in school. The teachers did notice, of course, but they were not very zealous either. He did learn to read and write, but as far as books go – he never cracked one open in his entire life.

On the other hand, in his teenage years, he got a touch of some unusual vanity that would later come back to haunt him. He was quite meticulous about his appearance and soon he began to slick back his blond hair. However, since at that time, in the villages, it was difficult to find brilliantine or something similar, Ponko decided to use simple soap for that purpose. Once, however, while walking around with his friends, it started to rain, and the soap on his slicked-back hair began to lather so much that it started running down his face and stinging his eyes. His friends wasted no time and promptly gave him a nickname – "Soaps". This rather mocking nickname quickly spread throughout the village, and from then on, everyone knew him as Ponko Soaps.

Overall, Ponko preferred to keep a distance from his friends and relatives. His personal life was a sort of a private domain. The only exception there was a friend of his, just one, coming from the same village, with whom he had served his time in the army. That friend's name was Stoycho, and in the autumn they both used to fill the wine barrels together, while the rest of the year they would go hunting.

After he was discharged from the army, Ponko married his neighbor, in a wedding that was both a love match and an arrangement between their parents. Stoyana, as the bride's name was, knew that Soaps had a difficult (or as they say in the countryside: "stubborn") character, but her time for marriage had come, and she was running out of options. The wedding was a modest affair, without much fuss. No white dresses, no expensive suits.

Ponko and Stoyana were people with strong leftist convictions. This was instilled in them by their families, who during the war secretly rooted for the Soviet victory. They attended organized meetings with the village youth, and at one such event Stoyana had a red scarf tied around her neck. That incident left a deep mark on her rustic mind, and that made her later see herself as a major player in the fight against fascism. In fact, one time, much later, she would even ask Ponko if she could claim official credit for her anti-fascist activities – after all, at that time, they were both candidate members of the early Komsomol, and they did tie a red scarf around *her* neck. This had infuriated Ponko, who looked at her and just gritted out through his teeth:

'Just look after your kids, woman!'

With that, Stoyana's aspirations had come to an end. It's worth mentioning that at that time they already had a son and a daughter.

Times were changing fast. After the "victory" of communism, the life of the whole country went into a completely new direction. With his rustic shrewdness, Ponko sensed the coming change and quickly moved to the nearby town, where he applied for a job in the militia. Soaps knew that a policeman would always get fed, while he also fancied the idea of being in charge of something. His entire childhood had been spent toiling away on the fields and among the livestock, so he invested all the strength and stamina he had, determined never to return to where he had come from. And he got it all.

Without a hitch, he passed the mandatory background check for joining the militia and thanks to the endorsements by some influential comrades, he was appointed a militia officer. After finishing a driving school, he was also assigned a brand new car – a red government Moskvich[4], with the caption "People's Militia" written on the side. That very day, his self-esteem soared. He used to

---

[4] *Moskvich:* A Soviet/Russian automobile brand produced by AZLK from 1946 to 1991. Later production has been resumed in Russia.

sit in the car with a stern expression on the face, maintaining the public order, always clean-shaven, with his hair inevitably combed back, to which he had added a thin, well-trimmed moustache. In short – this was a new, even reborn, Soaps.

To say that the police work satisfied him would have been an understatement. No, it did not simply satisfy him; it gave meaning to his otherwise empty life. And that was exactly the kind of people the new government was looking for – true believers, die-hard loyalists. They were the government's number one priority, at that stage way more important than people having proper education. In short, ideological tempering was the determining factor.

Soaps had become a staunch communist for a long time already. Joining the Communist Party had skyrocketed his career. In a short time, he rose to the office of head of a department in the militia. He worked day and night, relentlessly hunting down enemies of the state and anyone who dared disrupt the public order. It did not take him long to become known throughout the city as a man of unrelenting character who would not compromise with the law.

However, this much-desired promotion brought along not only satisfaction but also great disturbance and fear in Soaps' soul. He remained a half-educated man, after all, having never bothered to complete anything more than his eighth grade in school. He made frequent spelling mistakes when preparing his reports, and moreover

– even when writing down in his penalty notices the names of citizens, who had violated public order.

That was also a reason to buy a pocket dictionary, which he always carried with him, trying hard to keep it secret. With the little book always at hand, he made sure his spelling was always correct. But no matter how hard he tried to conceal it, his pocket dictionary did not escape the attention of his colleagues in the militia, and they began to mock and ridicule him behind his back. Occasionally, instead of calling him Soaps, they would even call him The Dictionary. All this only made Soaps even more peevish, taking it out on the drivers on the road who he used to stop and fine, as well as on the young people violating public order.

But despite those trifling aspects of our character's being, the Communist Party knew how to foster its loyal henchmen and take an overall care of them. What mattered most was that such a person just had to be *one of ours*; lack of education and merit was always excused. Subsequently, a large part of these newly arrived apparatchiks were sent to finish off their secondary education. Such was the evolution case of Soaps as well. For the Party, he was a loyal comrade who should be aided, since people like him were the backbone of communism, as a system.

Meanwhile, his wife Stoyana became a janitor at a school, but then Soaps arranged another job for her at the cannery as a shift supervisor. Stoyana was an industrious woman – that could not be denied. But alas, she lacked intelligence, or rather – education. After her husband got her a good job, she started to earn an even higher salary, which gave her the opportunity to set aside some money in a savings account. This had boosted her self-esteem so much that her colleagues found it difficult to even talk to her. But in Stoyana's mind, this new perspective was just the normal – even natural - way things should be. After all, she was a boss now, and her husband was a big shot – in the militia, no less.

Still, there's further room for our family to evolve, Stoyana sometimes thought. *The kids are growing up, but we're still living in a rented apartment.* But that was soon taken care of as well. It was not long before she and Soaps bought a two-room apartment, which would do for them for a while. That definitely brought some peace to Stoyana Ponkova's soul, and she began to feel the satisfaction in her life – imagine where she had come from and where she was now. She also had a posse of friends in the city. And those were not just any friends, but women of her status, wives of high local officials.

By the way, she enjoyed working at the cannery. Unlike her attitude towards her own subordinates, Stoyana knew how to butter up her bosses. So, she got along well with most of the management and even succeeded to get herself a bonus – a free trip to the Soviet Union. She traveled by train to Moscow and while there she bought two watches for her children and an iron for herself. Later, the family also got a brand new black and white TV.

Stoyana was well aware of her husband's harsh temper, so she always would cover up their children's mishaps. Soaps did not ever have a clue of their poor performance in school until they were already in high school, having established a sustainable pattern of poor grades. Stoyana knew this fact could have infuriated him and even make him beat them or else. But this never happened – Ponko was clueless, like a horse with blinders on. He had ceded everything to his wife – not just raising the kids, but an entire pile of family problems that he did not even suspect existed.

Soaps was completely consumed by his work and had already earned a reputation throughout the town as a stubborn nitpicker officer. All day long, even on weekends, he would lazily drive around town in his government Moskvich, idling on the roads, prowling for and eventually fining the wrongdoers. And that was how he ended up in an incident that would change his whole life.

On a Saturday evening, our character had stopped a truck at the town's exit. Ponko had noticed a serious traffic rules violation – one of the truck's headlights was out. Ponko was waving his traffic baton carelessly as he paced back and forth, inspecting the vehicle.

'Well, well…' Ponko began carpingly, in a squeaky voice, scratching the back of his neck. 'That's not how things happen, comrade! What are you doing driving with only one headlight? That's utter recklessness of you!'

Soaps pulled out a stack of ticket forms from the Moskvich and casually leaned on one side against the car trunk, propping himself on his elbow.

He lightly spat on his thumb to wet it and flipped open two blank forms, carefully placing an indigo sheet between them. Meanwhile, the truck driver paced anxiously around him, begging Ponko to spare him the ticket.

'But, comrade officer,' the driver whined like a kid, 'I've replaced that headlight… I did… just before the trip! I'm telling you the truth! No point lying to you, right?' he kept on asking rhetorically, hopping around Soaps. 'No idea why it's not working.'

But Soaps was inexorable, deaf to the driver's pleas. Eventually, exhausted, the driver made one last attempt to wangle something:

'Comrade officer, allow me to go… with one headlight… And tomorrow, first thing in the morning, in the workshop, we're gonna fix the entire electrical system of that truck.'

These words as if took Ponko out of the meditative trance he had fallen in while filling in the ticket form. He slowly turned around to the driver, giving him the once-over, and replied in his still squeaky voice:

'Such tricks don't work on me, comrade. Hand me over your driver's license and off to home!'

These were the last words that Sopas could later recall of that fateful evening. After he had tucked the offender's license into his pocket with smug satisfaction, he bent down to get back into the Moskvich. The truck driver seized the moment and slammed a heavy iron crank over his head. Then he snatched his license back and ran away.

Ponko awoke in the hospital the next day, disoriented and initially mistaking the doctor for a restaurant chef due to his white coat. His memories were hazy and took about a week to fully resurface. It turned out that after the driver had fled, passersby found Ponko, lying face down next to the Moskvich, and rushed him to the hospital.

The incident shattered Ponko's poise. He tried to keep his head up and go about his days like before, but the spark was gone. And then came another blow to his ego – after twenty years of service in the police force, he was retired without even being notified. This was the final straw. He fell into a deep depression and started having a glass of brandy and another glass of wine each and every evening. Forced into retirement far too young, he felt his entire life he had built with such dedication, was ripped away in a heartbeat.

Soaps realized that his time had gone by. His trusty government Moskvich was gone, as was his militia uniform – all the symbols behind his former authority. They did keep him on as a volunteer officer and did not take away his traffic baton, but he was no longer the feared militia officer – he was simply Ponko the pensioner.

In a couple of years certain changes occurred in Soaps' family. His son got married and then grandchildren came, which briefly pulled Ponko away from his grim reality. It was then that he and Stoyana decided to buy an apartment in the cooperative housing property on 3 Komsomolska Street. They were "expanding", so to speak.

Back in those days, their daughter secured a job in the capital and then got married there, so her visits became less frequent. Their son continued to live with them, together with his children, but not for long. Following the advent of democracy in the country, he left for Canada with his wife and children, in the very first wave of Bulgarian emigrants.

And so, Soaps and Stoyana were left to spend their retirement together, alone, in their apartment on Komsomolskaya Street, where, one could say, they felt comfortable. And this is the moment to explain a little more about how they had acquired that apartment. A few years before the end of communism, they bought it from Comrade Sivnev, who had also retired already, and – in his day

– had been a prominent anti-fascist activist. However, there was a small detail about the purchase that Stoyana kept concealed from her husband – something she did quite often though.

After that incident with the crank and his stay in the hospital, Soaps literally abdicated even the few things he had been involved in at home. He had left everything in his wife's hands, continuing to play the role of a horse with blinders on, albeit unconsciously. Nevertheless, he had complete confidence in her, never having doubted her actions throughout their marriage.

Therefore, the entire deal for the acquisition of the property on Komsomolska Street was orchestrated by Soaps's wife. Stoyana was cunning and shrewd enough, so she had sensed early on that Comrade Sivnev, despite his reputation as an honest communist and anti-fascist, was actually quite a greedy and unscrupulous one. Therefore, she had decided to offer him a win-win deal concluded through just a verbal agreement. The idea was to enter only the state-appraised price into the notary act for the acquisition of the property, meaning the money the state would have paid for the specific apartment, which was well below the price that Sivnev actually asked. This way, both parties would avoid paying hefty fees and taxes to the state for the ownership transfer. Afterwards, Stoyana proposed, they would pay off the rest of the money to Sivnev in cash, under the table. When Sivnev, a frail old man by then, heard her proposal, his eyes started gleaming with greed – he did not even hesitate but directly accepted the proposal. After all, both Soaps and Sivnev, and even Stoyana herself, were prominent local communist activists, so no one would even suspect the scam.

And so, it was done. The deal went smoothly, and everyone was satisfied. Soaps and Stoyana would move into a wonderful new apartment, while Comrade Sivnev would line his pockets with some cash. However, after signing the papers at the notary's office, a week or two went by, but yet, Sivnev did not receive the second half of the money as he had been promised. The old man started to worry, but he told himself that, after all, both parties were good old comrades and communists, so there was no room for worry, he would eventually get the outstanding amount. Except, a whole month went by, and there was still no news from Stoyana. Finally, the old anti-fascist activist gathered his courage and decided to call her to see what was going on and why they were so late with that cash. But alas, when he called, he got stunned. On the phone, Stoyana snapped at him that he had already gotten what he was due and that not a penny more would be paid to him, and then she slammed down the phone receiver. She knew it very well that Sivnev had acquired the apartment at the lower, state-appraised value, and that now he could not complain to anyone, since he himself was involved in the scam. And what was more – from a legal point of view, he would be deemed to have acquired even greater benefits from an actual crime. In short, Stoyana Ponkova did not keep her end of the bargain, and ultimately, she had acquired the apartment at a price significantly lower than the originally agreed-upon. All of this had happened behind Soaps's back, who had already started drinking heavily and throughout this episode was genuinely happy that they had bought a spacious apartment in a good location at a bargain price.

However, on that very day in September 2008, while Ponko was sitting on the bench to the right of the entrance of apartment building at number 3 on that very same Komsomolska Street, a stranger woman stopped in front of him, greeted him politely, and said in a serious tone:

'I'm the daughter of Comrade Sivnev, the one that you bought your apartment from. My father passed away but before that he told me how you had deceived him and had not paid him the money for the apartment, as had been agreed – the agreement was only verbal though, so you swindled him, after all. I've just come to inform you that he left this world deeply disappointed by you.'

Soaps was staring at her, standing numb in one place. He felt his heart started pounding, and his face flushed while a wave of dizziness washed over him. He tried to stand up, propping on his cane, but failed to do so and sat back down. It was the first time he heard about those things ever. He did not know what to say; it was too much for him to bear. He bowed his head and wept bitterly. He found the strength to only utter:

'I'm sorry… I … didn't know…'

But the woman did not wait for his answer and left.

Soaps spent the entire day on the bench, utterly exhausted by the accusations. He felt like he had been tossed aside like garbage. In the evening, he tried to talk to Stoyana about the matter, but she just curtly replied that to pay everything to Sivnev was not a rightful thing to do, that old rogue who had lived off his past laurels all his life, and for sure was not much of an anti-fascist activist after all. Then the old woman quickly left the room and went to wash the dishes.

Ponko Soaps was alone. His aged mind was reeling, flummoxed. It was like his entire life was screened before him, like a movie reel. Memories of the militia, his government Moskvich, the relentless pursuit of injustice and deceit – all came flooding back. And now – at the twilight of his life – he realized that these very evils had been lurking all around him, seemingly invisible but to his eyes only. His entire world – everything he had believed in and fought for – had crumbled in an instant. The foundations of his soul had been shattered. *We were supposed to be communists,* Soaps thought bitterly. *But all along, it has turned out I've been nothing but a fool!*

MAMA NEDA AND HER SON

His father, Ivan, was a good man, earning his honest living through twelve hours of hard labor, each and every day. He worked as a watchman at the town's oil mill, and it was a job that suited him just fine. He earned enough to provide for his family. Day and night, he patrolled the oil mill's premises, familiar with every worker's face. He kept a watchful eye for infractions, and if he noticed any, he personally reported them to the owner, Iliya Penchev.

Penchouloo, as everybody used to nickname Iliya Penchev, had added a small outside room attached to the building of the oil mill where the family of Ivan, the watchman, was accommodated. Ivan had married recently, although the young couple had no children yet. He was a decent fellow, but he had failed to find true love. His father arranged a quick marriage, and Ivan first met his bride on the day of the engagement party. When he was introduced to her, he thought that she was not the kind of woman he had expected his parents to pick for him, but eventually he yielded and settled into married life. Nevertheless, he did the right thing, or at least he did what was expected of him. He did not oppose, so he and his wife moved out of his father's house soon after the wedding.

Neda, his wife, didn't have a job and was a stay-at-home type. She would spend her days in the room, cooking and cleaning, and after finishing her chores, she would take a stroll around the oil mill. She was in her early twenties, plump, of average height, and full of energy. She had a domineering personality and could be rude and pushy at times. She could not tolerate dissent and always did what she pleased. Moreover, she was quite clever and unscrupulous.

Ivan quickly realized Neda's true nature, but – to his regret – he had no way out. The wedding had been a lavish affair, with plenty of music, noise, and good food. His father had spent a small fortune and was not about to tolerate any complaints coming from his son. Besides, in the small town they were living in, a divorce was an unthinkable taboo. So, for now, let's say the new couple did not separate; or rather, they would separate, but it happened much later and not by choice, but rather due to tragic circumstances. For now, let's go on with our story and return to their life after the wedding.

Neda enjoyed sitting on the bench in front of her little room at the oil mill and she would not let anyone pass by without thoroughly questioning them. She sought out conversations with anyone who would walk by her, and in these brief chats she always tried to show how smart, beautiful, and resourceful she was, and how her husband was the one who actually "benefited" from their marriage, and that their love knew no limits.

With Ivan's first paycheck following the wedding, Neda indulged herself in two new dresses and a pair of high heels that were trending at the time. Despite having spent the first two decades of her life in the countryside, she began dressing and styling herself like an urban woman, and she rather relished that transformation. Should someone look at her face for some time longer, he would notice her eyes flitting from one man to the next. And so, it was not long before Neda turned her attention to the owner of the oil mill, Mr. Penchouloo. It should be noted that these events took place in the 1930s, when any such flirtations with older, well-off men would be met with fierce social disapproval and rejection.

Mr. Penchouloo was a bulky man about his fifties, always impeccably dressed in a suit and tie. He invariably wore a black bowler hat on his head, and his shoes were always elegant, bought sometime during his trips to Europe. He adhered to a strict daily routine of bathing and shaving, always carrying the subtle fragrance of cologne around him. In short, he was a sophisticated man.

Penchouloo was a man of amorous adventures. He was notorious throughout the town as a womanizer, and his flirtations with young moms were no secret to anyone. But he made sure to "compliment" the daughters of older ladies as well. Barely a week had passed since Ivan's wedding, and Mr. Penchev had already noticed his wife, being far from indifferent. On the contrary, all sorts of lustful thoughts began running through his head.

During that period, the oil mill business was running well. There were profits, and Penchouloo used to pay the workers' salaries just on time. There were no worries about production and sales, and such stability of the enterprise, in turn, gave him freedom and time to indulge in love affairs and flirtations.

In the moments when Penchouloo's thoughts would turn to Neda, he would purse his lips, acknowledging she was a bit chubby, but then he would gulp, chuckle and shake those thoughts off his head. After all, he was not a spring chicken either. So, the timing for a potential affair with the young peasant woman could not have come better.

The relationship with that woman, however, turned out to be a double-edged sword and everything was hastily brought to an end. Neda began scrounging money for clothes, shoes, and even food from him. Yet, Penchouloo was not that kind of man. He used to earn his money for his family's sake, not for hers, and he was paying her husband a fair salary as well. Nevertheless, he had put an end to their affair early on, Neda kept on soliciting miscellaneous things from him, and this irritated him greatly. Finally, Iliya Penchev began to bitterly regret that he had ever started this meaningless fling, and after a couple of months he fired Ivan. Eventually, the young family found themselves out of both the oil mill and the small room there.

Soon afterwards, Neda gave birth to a boy, but she was not sure whether the father was her husband, Ivan, or Penchouloo. The child was healthy and strong. They named him Kolyo, and the more he grew, the more his resemblance to Mr. Penchev became apparent. Neda secretly hoped that the kid's real father would recognize him and claim him an heir. However, this never happened. Several times she attempted to reach the owner of the oil mill and ask for money, but all was in vain. Penchouloo started to avoid her, and so everything finally ended.

Ivan never found out about his wife's infidelity and he continued to cherish his family devotedly. Eventually, Neda gave birth to their second son, and Ivan bought a plot of land and built a family house. Such was their life when the events of September 9, 1944 unfolded, and the Soviet Army entered the country, marking the beginning of the communist era in Bulgaria. In their small town, everything happened so quickly that people did not even realize how the political power had changed hands. Shortly after that, Ivan was mobilized by the army and sent to the front, where he perished in a war that he knew almost nothing about, leaving behind him two orphan kids.

After the family had suffered this terrible loss, Kolyo, the elder son who had already grown up, realized that it was now about time for him to take care of his mother and younger brother. The money his father used to earn was gone, and his mother never took a proper job. Young Kolyo had inherited Neda's unscrupulousness and greed, as well as the ability to sniff out money from afar. He committed two thefts from the store of a village cooperative and then sold the loot at half price to friends and relatives. Under pressure from his mother, he broke into the oil mill's safe and took all he found inside. Neda had told him that Penchouloo kept a lot of money there. Incidentally, when Kolyo committed this robbery, even though it was in the middle of the night, Penchouloo saw him in the yard of the mill but kept quiet, and even later, he never spoke a word about that. After all, the boy was his son, illegitimate though.

But even this money soon depleted, forcing Kolyo to sell their father's land to keep the family fed. After some time, things got a bit easier as his younger brother took off for Germany, at the age of fifteen, joining some traveling circus actors, and eventually settled there. No one ever saw the young man again. He would only send small packages with gifts for New Year to his mother and his elder brother.

By this time, Kolyo had already entered his prime. A real looker, he had jet-black hair, always perfectly slicked back with hair gel. His face had matured into that of a grown man. He liked to be clean-shaven and wore dark sunglasses. He was just as particular about his clothes, always making sure his pants were pressed perfectly, while his white shirts were washed and ironed by his mother on a daily basis. The girls in the town liked him and many of them had become sort of his admirers. It did not take long for him to distinguish himself as a womanizer and people nicknamed him The Ram as he was rather brash, and this last quality was largely the foundation of his success among women. Kolyo was well aware that women were attracted to him. Unfortunately, he had no money. Eventually, he realized that no matter how brazen he was, he would still be poor and ultimately he would fail to meet the eventual material needs of more sophisticated young ladies. And this thought greatly depressed him.

That period marked the beginning of the nationalization of private property and the establishment of collective farms, similar to the Soviet kolkhozes. Kolyo could not quite wrap his head around the new reality evolving in the country, so it was his mother's turn to take charge of the family's survival. So, Neda forced him to join the Komsomol, the youth organization of the communist party. And as it turned out this was an actual breakthrough moment for him. Very soon, this young, uneducated, and pilferage-inclined man found his footing and began running various initiatives locally.

During those years the communists began laying the foundations of their ruling system – and in particular it was the establishment of the communists' nomenklatura at both local and national level. Kolyo's spotless record made him a perfect fit for the new regime, which placed him at the forefront of the new government bureaucracy. His working-class origins and the fact that his father had died a war hero gave him impeccable credentials. This helped him secure the position of Komsomol secretary of the town, which marked the beginning of a successful career in the Communist-Party-led state. His full membership in the Communist party was just the final and natural step up in his career.

Nationalization was at its peak, and the old oil mill was no exception. Penchouloo, a man now in his twilight years, was branded an enemy of the people and sent to a labour camp, and in this Neda played a key part. Fueled by years of resentment, she instigated her unsuspecting son to make sure his real father was sent to a labor camp, where he would never return from.

Kolyo's life kept on unfolding smoothly, as if guided by some unseen hand. Then, fate intervened and he encountered the beautiful Emma near the Girls High School in town. That blonde beauty, with her slender figure, captivated the young suitor's heart for good. Having grown up in a rural setting, Emma's father had ambitious plans for his daughter, intending to educate her and find her a suitable husband in town.

Nearly eighteen, Emma was a blossoming beauty at that time. In addition to her elegant figure, she enchanted Kolyo with her refined manners. She was an excellent cook, and she was also keen about books. Emma lived in a rented flat which she shared with another girl, and every Sunday she went to the bus station, where an appointed man from her village would arrive, carrying food parcels for all the young people from the village who were studying in the town. This way, her father would send her supplies for the entire week, but there were no indulgences. Emma excelled in her studies and graduated from high school without difficulty.

Their romance blossomed swiftly and seamlessly. Kolyo and Emma fell deeply in love, thus forging a new family. Though her father, a small-scale farmer, disapproved of Kolyo, he was powerless to intervene. After the wedding, Kolyo received generous support from his father-in-law and stopped pilfering. Dedicated to his newly found family, he became a devoted husband. Unaware of Kolyo's previous life, Emma completed an engineering degree via a part-time university programme, which was a highly appreciated qualification during the early years of communism and industrialization.

Unlike Emma, since his childhood, science had never had any appeal to Kolyo. It was precisely his lack of education that was about to break his career. But the Communist Party was taking care of its people, and Kolyo was already part of the communist nomenklatura, whom they valued. Eventually, an influential comrade from the town's party committee recommended him for manager of an enterprise providing miscellaneous services to the people living in the town. And Kolyo liked this job. The enterprise employed various specialists – from machine technicians, electricians, welders, plumbers, to television technicians, and above all of them, at the top of the hierarchy, Kolyo was the boss. The main activity of the enterprise was related to services in private homes and government institutions. Thus, in the blink of an eye, in the hands of Kolyo, this young man, loyal to the party, were given quite a bit of power and resources. He was the one who distributed bonuses to the employees of the enterprise and who signed orders for hiring or firing workers.

Kolyo enjoyed attending various assignments together with his subordinates, especially going to beer-and-grill joints that used to pop up like mushrooms during the communist era. He turned these visits into a time for relaxation and good food. Of all things, most of all he enjoyed the repairs to the grills for roasting meatballs and kebabs. But it was precisely one such visit that would cast a shameful stain on his biography.

That day, Kolyo and two of his electricians responded to a call from a small restaurant about a grill there not working. The appliance had not been functioning since that morning, while the place was always busy, with lots of customers coming mostly to order a plate of meatballs or kebabs and grab a beer or two. It turned out that the problem with the grill was a burned-out relay. The technicians quickly figured out what was wrong and immediately replaced the damaged part. But they still needed to test the appliance before leaving, and what better way to test a grill than grilling some meatballs on it? Kolyo took on this task, called over the restaurant manager, her name was Vasilka, and said:

'Vaska, let's grill some meat balls to make sure everything goes fine.'

Of course, the woman followed his orders, and so began – let's say – an unusual test of the grill's functionality. They tossed one meatball after another onto the grill until, finally, Kolyo had eaten eleven ones. Vasilka watched, bewildered as our hero greedily devoured that whole pile of meat. She was deeply offended but said nothing. She knew Kolyo well and was aware that should she say a word, he might not send a team so fast to repair a broken grill next time and that could result in spoiling some meat and significant losses for the restaurant. After the team had "certified" themselves that the appliance was working, they got into their company car and left.

However, that very same day, on her way home, Vasilka ran into Kolyo's wife, whom she had known for many years. They exchanged a few words, and Vasilka, casually, as if just making a conversation, asked Emma:

'Hey, Emma, did Kolyo have lunch at home today?'

'Yes,' Emma replied to the odd question. 'Why are you asking?'

'Oh, it's nothing...' Vasilka replied in a sly tone. 'It's just that they were fixing the grill at the restaurant today, as he went ahead and ate eleven meatballs. I'm not saying anything, Emma... I was just worried he might feel sick.'

Those words hurt Emma deeply. As if a knife had pierced her heart. She was so offended. She remembered how Kolyo had come home during his lunch break and eaten two plates of moussaka[5] and did not even look full.

Emma was a calm person by nature and did not like having arguments. However, this evening she could not contain her indignation and the insult she felt because of her husband's behaviour. The children took the side of their mother. Such a scandal broke out for the first time in their home. Kolyo felt that his authority, as the pillar of this family and an honest man, was dangerously shaken, while he cared deeply about his clean moral image before his children. This woman, Vasilka, had humiliated him in front of Emma and the kids, made him a fool and pathetic. And he conceived a plan for revenge, 'I'm gonna get even with her. I just need to find her soft spot.'

---

[5] *Moussaka* – an eggplant (aubergine) or potato-based dish, often including ground meat, which is common in the Balkans and the Middle East. *(Source: Wikipedia)*

That same evening, he went to his mother's place to tell her about the derisible situation he had been put in. Neda, who was approaching sixty at that time, spent the whole day on the bench in front of her house, just as she once used to do at the oil mill. She would constantly keep an eye on who was going where and never missed a chance to start a conversation with anyone passing by. That's how she had found out that Nelly, Vasilka's daughter, was an agronomist and was in charge of the demonstration garden to the town's school. According to Neda, this same Nelly was illicitly taking fruits and vegetables from there.

The demonstration garden was about one acre in size. There, the school students – little builders of communism – learned work habits by planting vegetables and fruit trees, and then cultivating, watering, and caring for them. Though small in size, this field produced a significant amount of fruits and vegetables year-round, depending on the season. There was even a quarter of an acre planted with wheat and barley. Nelly was quite skilled at her work and often got praise for her efforts. It was likely that some of the produce from the demonstration garden was eventually sold, but this was not a topic of discussion at that time. Generally, during the communist era, the students' labor on the garden was unpaid, or if any money was given out at all, it was merely symbolic.

Kolyo's mother had noticed that whenever Nelly would pass by her on her way home, she always carried a yellow plastic bucket, apparently full of something. However, the bucket was carefully covered with an old copy of the "Rabotnichesko Delo"[6] daily. 'Most likely, the bucket is full of fruits and vegetables from the demonstration garden,' Neda had concluded. But that was only a guess, as no one had ever seen the contents of the mysterious yellow bucket.

However, Nelly's husband was a high-ranking member of the Communist Party in the town, and therefore checking the contents of the bucket was unthinkable – this was how things happened at that time. But there was one fact that could not be concealed: the crumpled copy of the "Rabotnichesko Delo" daily that was used to cover the contents of the bucket. This was now an actual cause for concern, and Kolyo raised the case for discussion before a party meeting, just a couple of days after the eleven-meatball episode.

'Look, comrades!' he said. 'I'm not claiming Nelly is stealing produce from the demonstration garden. I'm concerned about something far more troubling, and it is: "Rabotnichesko Delo", the daily, the printed voice of our party, is being used to cover buckets.' He finished with a worried expression.

Then, other party members took the floor and claimed they had actually seen Nelly carrying cherries in the bucket. Some said it

---

[6] *Rabotnichesko Delo (Workers' Feat)* – The official daily of the Bulgarian Communist Party at that time.

was not cherries but cucumbers, and so on and so forth. Eventually, Nelly was dismissed from her office. Although, due to her husband's influence, she was reinstated after two or three months.

Kolyo was satisfied. He felt he had gotten his revenge, and gleefully spread the story throughout the town, giving fiery speeches about how everyone should be uncompromising when it came to theft and lawlessness. None of the ordinary people dared to oppose. Everyone knew these were squabbles among party comrades, and no one could have predicted how it would end.

A few years later, on a cold winter night just before New Year's Eve, two high school students found Kolyo lying on the street in front of the workshop where he worked. He was covered in blood and mumbling incoherently. Someone had hit him on the head, with a heavy object obviously, and he was bleeding profusely. His left eye was swollen, closed, and bruised. They immediately called an ambulance and he was taken to the district hospital. Several head surgeries followed, but he never fully recuperated.

After he was discharged from the hospital, he had difficulty walking and his right hand remained paralyzed. It was never discovered who had done this to him. An investigation was conducted, but nothing came out of it. Rumors circulated around town that the most likely perpetrator was Nelly's husband, but these were just speculations and guesses.

Kolyo saw the coming of democracy confined to a wheelchair, with half of his body paralyzed. He was certified as disabled, though he got just a meager pension. His mother passed away shortly after the incident, and he was left in the care of his wife, Emma, who never left his side and continued to love him with all her heart.

THE GALABOVS FAMILY'S RIGHTNESS

Tolinchevo was a small town in Southern Bulgaria, just a 40-minute drive inland from the seaside. It was situated in a picturesque plain framed by soft rolling hills.

In those days, the town boasted a well-defined central area, dominated by the imposing gray building of the people's community center. The entire ground floor of the building was taken by a spacious hall, capable of seating nearly five hundred people, and it was the venue for a wide range of public events. Communist Party meetings, as well as various planned gatherings of its sister organization like the Komsomol or the Fatherland Front[7] were all regular fixtures on its calendar.

Sometimes the town would be graced by visits of popular folk music and dance ensembles of that time, which the people of Tolinchevo passionately adored, vastly attending their performances. During such events, the hall would be sold out, but people would

---

[7] *Fatherland Front*: A Bulgarian pro-communist political resistance movement, which began in 1942 during World War II. Later on, during the Communist Era in the country, it was turned into a sister party to the ruling Communist Party, used by the communists to simulate a multi-party system and democracy.

nevertheless come, standing up for hours or sitting on the steps just to applaud their favorite singers and dancers. Once or twice a year, the stage would also host the musicians of the symphony orchestra and opera singers from the district town, and the locals would eagerly immerse themselves in the divine sounds of the music of Mozart, Beethoven, or enjoy some of Rossini's operas.

The second floor was home to an extensive library, divided into two sections – the first one, at the start of the corridor, was a smaller area catered to the younger readers, while the second one, twice as large, housed an impressive collection of adult fiction and a vast number of popular science books.

On the left side of the community center perched the newly erected building of the Communist Party Town Committee, while parallel to it the large Orthodox Holy Trinity church rose up. Beyond it, a row of shops lined both sides of the main street. This architecture would later change significantly on its own, after the advent of democracy, as most of the shops went bankrupt, and others were closed. In the end, they were all demolished, and the entire space was transformed into a magnificent park with fountains and some futuristic statues, whose meaning the people of Tolinchevo never found, nor did they ever get to know the names of those who had sculpted them or what that particular art was doing in their park at all.

A long alleyway stretched on from the heart of the city – or rather from the community center building. It was about two hundred meters long by thirty meters wide, flanked by towering trees. In the middle, along its entire length, there was a flower bed with roses of all colours, surrounded by rows of carefully planted dandelions. Both sides of the *boulevard*, as the people of Tolinchevo affectionately referred to the alley, were lined with benches which were occupied almost around the clock by the locals who loved to gather there, eager to share views and opinions on news and politics.

Going back in time, during the period that followed the "victory" of communism, we can say that the town experienced a rapid growth thanks to the numerous people flocking in from the adjacent villages. Here, they could easily find jobs in the new industrial plants and factories where a diverse range of products was manufactured – from bolts and nuts to canned vegetables. Industrialization had begun, and Tolinchevo was not an exception from this trend. At the same time, new grocery stores called *gastronomes* sprang up, the butcher shops were expanded, and a new public bathhouse was built. Here it is important to mention that new schools were built too, during that period.

The town featured its own distinctive and fascinating way of life. It enjoyed a magnificent climate as well. The mornings in the summer were especially pleasant – at noon, it became warm, but not hot, and in the afternoons, you could feel the breeze coming from the sea, which the locals here used to call the *Mariner*. The winters were mild, and snow rarely lingered. Spring was lush and beautiful, while only autumn could rival it, which was like gold, or if it happened to be rainy, then the greenery lasted longer and beauty spread as far as the human eye could see.

In the summer, most of the people of Tolinchevo used to spend their vacations at the seaside, while others preferred the mountains. The trade unions had created a well-organized system, thanks to which people from the working class could spend the vacations with their families at low prices in fairly decent sanatoriums, bungalows, or private apartments. To the people of Tolinchevo, the large luxury complexes, such as Sunny Beach and Golden Sands, still remained out of reach, although it was not only because of the high prices. The thought that they would cough up as much money as a Western European tourist for a vacation, was just unbearable to them. It was simply the people's mentality of the time. So, people used to find miscellaneous and creative ways to provide for the vacations of their families – they would either go to the so-called *trade union rest homes*, or stay with friends and relatives, thus saving money while enjoying the company of people they felt close to.

The people of Tolinchevo stood out by their diligence and, among other things, they had planted vineyards on the hills surrounding the city, tilling and cultivating them assiduously.

Autumn was a special time in the lives of the male citizens of the town, as it marked the beginning of the grape harvest, followed by the distillation of homemade rakia[8] and the making of homemade wine. Rakia was distilled in stills, and wine was aged in barrels. In this small provincial town this was not just a tradition – people were deeply convinced that the rakia and the wine they used to make were superior to those made by the state-owned wineries, and of course, it all came much cheaper to them.

However, all that romantic tradition of alcohol homemaking, deeply rooted in local folklore, was occasionally disrupted by visits from the state tax officials. During the communist era, they used to conduct regular inspections to account for the quantity of the alcohol produced. These occasions would always result in frantic efforts to hide the excess output, produced over the allowed limits, in attics and basements. Furthermore, there were some people who succeeded to somehow make some money on the black market. They, in turn, had to stash their finances anywhere in the house – for instance, burying them beneath the floor of the garage or the cellar.

Beyond these particular details, life in Tolinchevo followed a rather monotonous and predictable rhythm, dictated by the changing seasons.

---

[8] *Rakia*: A traditional Bulgarian brandy typically produced from grapes or other fruits.

Such was the general background, outlined by laws – some written, some not, that the Galabovs led their life in. Donyo Galabov and Svetoslava had married shortly after the communists' "victory". Svetoslava was a local, born in Tolinchevo, and her father, Georgi, was a shoemaker who had carried on a long family tradition of shoemaking. He made his shoes in a tiny tin shed with its door always open while he was working. The whole town knew him and everybody opted for his services in case a pair of tattered shoes needed mending.

Driven by his bourgeois attitudes, Georgi was doing his best to provide a good education for his only daughter. He bought her an accordion and a violin. However, at that time, in that small town, there was no one to teach her the violin, so she started taking accordion lessons. Later on, Svestolava graduated from a library studies institute and began working at the town's library. She was a charming and kind woman, loved by the people of their neighborhood and the entire town. She was of average height, with curly black hair and bright, greenish eyes, smiling all the time – or most of the time, at least.

Donyo had been born and raised in a village, working in the fields since he had been a little boy. He helped his father to raise livestock and spent summers herding sheep. His father had decided that was the best for his son and regularly skipped sending him to school. Nevertheless, Donyo was a diligent schoolboy and was ambitious too, so he graduated eighth grade having learned to read and write properly. Before September 9 1944, he never quite mustered the courage to become a member of WYL[9], the secret organization of the communist youth, although he was always hanging around them to learn something.

He was a handsome young man, tall and well-built. Years of working in the fields had contributed to his strong and fit physique. He had jet-black hair, combed back, and made quite an impression on young women. Every girl wanted to dance with him at the *soirées*, as they called the social gatherings of young people at that time. At one such gathering, he met his future wife, Svetoslava. They fell in love – at first sight, as they say – and got married soon after that.

Then, Donyo moved from the village to the city and quite soon realized that his eighth-grade only education could hardly get him a good job. So, he enrolled in the high school which he graduated from three years later. However, even the high school education turned out to be not high enough, and he would poignantly realize that fact when he failed to qualify for the position of district station head at the state post office services.

Donyo was utterly devoted to studying, but he was also well aware of the fact that he lacked the regular schooling he had been omitting while working with his father in the village. As a child, he

---

[9] *WYL*: Workers Youth League – communist youth organization from 1928 to 1947.

had no choice, but now, when everything depended on him only, he decided not to give up so easily.

A dream had long been taking roots in his mind, one that never left him. With all his heart, he desired to study economics – perhaps not so much to become an economist, but rather for the joy that the process of studying used to bring him. He often imagined himself attending lectures, taking notes on everything the professor would say, then taking exams with other students, and finally receiving his diploma. Therefore, even though he was well into his twenties, he secretly bought math textbooks for the high school classes and diligently solved math problems in the evenings.

Later, he made several attempts to enroll at the university, but he always failed on the admission exams, receiving low scores only. Certainly, it was just his wife who knew about these failures, but in the end, his dream of studying and becoming an economist remained unfulfilled. This left a deep mark on his soul that would never fade away with the years. Even in his old age, Donyo bitterly recalled all those sleepless nights he had spent leaning over the textbooks.

Meanwhile, during these years, he became the father of two daughters. His wife continued to work at the town library, but her salary was very low and the money was hardly enough for the family. And Donyo was devoted to his family and loved his wife and children immensely. He subordinated all his thought and action to them only, endeavoring to ensure some stability in their lives. Therefore, he pulled himself together a bit and began to look around for a job. Finally, he heard from a friend that the local slaughterhouse was looking for someone with a driving license for the distribution of meat and sausages. Donyo had a driving license and his biography was impeccable, but nevertheless, just in case, he asked his father-in-law, who was a member of the Communist Party, to intercede for him with the workshop manager. A few days after submitting his application, the manager's secretary contacted him and told him that he had been approved for the position.

From that day on, Donyo turned a new page in his life. He started getting up early and shaving every day, then putting on cheap cologne, getting dressed in a black suit, always with a perfectly pressed crease on the trousers, a crisp white shirt, and an invariably black tie with a pre-tied knot. As soon as he reached the meat processing factory, he would take off his jacket and put on a blue shop coat, then begin loading the truck with crates of meat, mince and sausages. The entire work process took place under the watchful eye of the workshop manager, and there was no possibility whatsoever for any pilfering or squandering. Then he would leave the workshop in the truck, turn left, and stop on the weighbridge at the gate – there, a second check of the quantity and type of sausages was carried out. Everything was weighed and recorded in invoices.

From the gate, the truck would then head to the town stores to make the deliveries.

So, the months were passing, while all that Donyo could do was watch jealously as meat, filets, and sausages were loaded and unloaded, without him being able to set anything aside for home – for his family. The control seemed strict, as the products were weighed and checked three times – in the workshop, at the workshop gate, and finally, in the store. In short, not even a chop of pork could be touched. Sometimes the workshop manager would give him a baton of sausage, but this rather occurred exceptionally, usually when a holiday was coming. And thefts were punished severely – with a job dismissal or an investigation by the Economic Police.

Before taking this job, Donyo hoped that he would be able to buy cheap meat and sausages from the meat processing plant, which would offset the low salary, but it turned out to be impossible or rather pointless, as the prices both in the plant and in the stores were the same. Then, his mind started working frantically. Sleep eluded him as he thought about how he could take something out of the plant and remain unnoticed and without being caught stealing. And he did not have to think long…

The opportunity came up unexpectedly. One day, Donyo was left alone in the mince room, waiting for the manager. But the manager was busy elsewhere, and suddenly Donyo felt a strong impulse that he was unable to resist. He looked over his shoulder a couple of times and, convinced that there was no one around, without much hesitation, he grabbed a handful of pork mince and stuffed it into one of the pockets of his black trousers. Cold sweat broke out on his forehead and on his back, and his heart started racing. He ducked slightly and looked around once more. *No one's here*, he thought encouragingly, and a sarcastic smile appeared on his face. Then a second impulse seemed to strike his consciousness as he instinctively reached into the crate of mince, grabbed as much as he could, and stuffed just another lump into the other pocket. Then he quickly buttoned up his blue shop coat and patted his thighs so that the bulging pockets would not expose him. A couple of minutes later, the workshop manager appeared.

'Come on, Donyo, let's get loading, they've held me up there with some invoices,' he called out cheerfully, unaware of the theft just perpetrated.

They loaded the mince onto the truck and our character set off to supply it to the stores. However, throughout the journey, he felt restless. Some kind of conscience spoke up inside him, and his mood became gloomy. He began feeling guilty for the disgraceful act he had committed.

How could I sink so low – to steal mince like the lowest of the low? How will I look others in the eye from now on? But this idea gradually began to fade away, as inside his mind he managed to find excuses – just satisfactory enough – for his deed. *I've done nothing wrong at all. I'm honest enough with everyone*, he was justifying his doing, as he was carrying the crates of minced meat. *The manager has never given me even a kilogram of mince, although he knows I have two children. He only throws me some measly batons of sausage... like I'm a dog or what?* But just when he decided that he had stolen the mince rightfully, a terrifying thought pierced his brain. *I just hope they are not going to notice... should they find out... then I'm screwed...* He felt faint, his stomach churned. *Dismissal... but dismissal is the least of it. Then the Economic Police, then State Security. What have I gotten myself into! They'll probably put me in prison... And what did I need that mince for, anyway? What for, damn it! I just hope they won't notice. I'll probably be beaten in prison. And what about the children? They'll say their father is a criminal – and that's the end... just the end!* After all that heart-wrenching inner struggle, Donyo hurried back to the workshop as quickly as possible. He wanted to find out if anyone had suspected anything. The sweat on his back had soaked through his blue shop coat, forming a large wet stain.

After he had parked the truck in the workshop, he quickly jumped out on the ground and headed towards the mince room, pretending nothing had happened. He walked lightly and casually, listening carefully, when a familiar voice suddenly pulled him out of his trance and he jumped, startled.

'Hey, Donyo, you've been running or what? You're sweating buckets!'

Donyo turned around and saw the manager's mocking face.

That's it... it's all over... the bastard knows everything, Donyo thought, feeling as if he would cry. His mouth was dry, but he managed to keep his composure as much as he could and replied with a crooked smile:

'Me? Running? Why? It's very hot today, Comrade Manager. And those crates I've been carrying around, they've really taken a toll on me,' he said this last part, trying to evoke any kind of response from the manager, so he could find out if they had discovered the theft.

'Stop complaining, boy,' the manager called out cheerfully, 'you're still young, and if you only knew how many crates you'll have to carry yet...' and he passed by, patting Donyo on the shoulder.

They haven't discovered it, Donyo was almost whining with relief inside his mind. *Ha! Fools! Of course, there's no way they can catch me – after all, I'm much smarter than them.* He felt relieved and hurried home to enjoy his loot. All his recent dark thoughts, which had nearly led him to frenzy, had gone.

But only when he got home, he realized what a stupid thing he had done. His pants and underwear were greasy, and the mince had stuck to the fabric, so eventually he could barely salvage anything fit for cooking. *It's good the pants are black. Otherwise, they would have caught me by now,* Donyo concluded in his thoughts. But this was not a failure for him. Because with this failure came also the solution to the problem. He could not fall asleep that night and eventually he decided that he needed new pants – not just one pair, but two. The next day he went to a tailor and ordered two pairs of black pants with a higher waist and cuffs, specifically asking they be wider in the hips. The tailor was a little surprised but said nothing. He took Donyo's measurements and accepted the order.

A week later, Donyo already had two pairs of brand new black pants with the desired cut. However, the plan did not end there. He called his wife and together they unseamed the pockets. Then Donyo took a few sturdy nylon bags and had her sew them to the inside of the pockets so he could safely hide therein whatever he got his hands on at the processing plant. Svetoslava got very scared as she felt that this was wrong, but she loved him unconditionally and would do anything for him. And not least of all, she also realized that they had two children to feed. So she did as Donyo told her and sewed the additional dark nylon bags as instructed.

This was a turning point in the history of the Galabovs. From that day on, Donyo began to lurk around the processing plant even more often, and when he would find himself alone, he would sneak whatever he could into his pockets – meat, mince, or sausages. The years were going by, but no one suspected that this seemingly refined man, always dressed in a suit and clean-shaven, with neatly combed hair, an impeccable biography, and a solid rural background, was committing the most basic of low acts, every single day. People, especially women, loved to stop him on the street, exchanging a couple of words with this refined gentleman, without the slightest suspicion of his thefts from the plant's production. Production that was – in itself – theirs, it was property of the people. It was communism, after all!

Sometimes the nylon pockets would rip and the pants would get greasy, and then Svetoslava had to wash them by hand because they did not have a washing machine. But she would wisely not hang them out to dry in the yard during the day, as a precaution against curious neighbors. The woman would wait until evening came and only when she was convinced it was dark enough she would go and hang up the pants. Then, early in the morning, before dawn, she would hurry to take them down before anyone saw them.

Donyo's plan worked flawlessly, and for years he would provide meat and quality sausages for his family. Svetoslava only had to go to the local grocery store from time to time to buy a piece of sausage to quell any suspicion. The Galabovs' children took all this for granted and eagerly waited for their father to come home in the evenings and start taking various delicious stuff out of his pockets.

Incidentally, after Donyo's scheme had started working, he even began to set aside some savings. This allowed him to vacation at spa resorts for two weeks every summer. The intriguing aspect of that case was that he always went there alone, without taking his wife or children with him. As an excuse, Donyo told his wife that he went to the spa because his back ached from hard work, and that he went alone because he wanted to get rid of all that stress accumulated at the meat plant. In reality, however, the reason was rather different. Donyo was a handsome man and, as we've already said, women were particularly fond of him, while he knew how to charm them. That's why his choice of spa resorts as vacation spots was no coincidence. Usually, ladies from all over the country would flock to such places, many of whom were alone too – or at least that's how they looked. So, Donyo had the opportunity to enjoy short-lived romances with some of the female visitors there, every summer. Svetoslava had her doubts about her husband's affairs, however she was always quick to dismiss such thoughts from her head, trying to convince herself that her husband was really quite stressed, thus deserving some break from his woes at work.

Years passed imperceptibly, and Donyo reached retirement age. No one ever revealed his secret – he was never caught red-handed. On the contrary, he was held up as a role model among his colleagues. And eventually, he felt satisfied that he had been providing good food for his family. Sometimes he wanted to brag, to share his experience, because he had not heard of anyone else stealing likewise. All he was left with was the concealed satisfaction and pride in his ingenuity and that he had managed to deceive everyone in the plant, yet remaining unpunished. People would see him as an elegant man, dressed in a suit and a tie, with polished shoes, honest and respectable. A man who worked from dawn till dusk to feed his family. Other women held him up as a pattern to be followed by their husbands.

What else could I do?, Donyo would sometimes ponder; his mind had come up with what those times required. Sometimes he would laugh in his sleep, and in the morning his wife would ask him what he was laughing about, and he would proudly reply, 'I fooled everyone with that meat in the plant, and no one ever figured it out.' After all, he was just one cunning peasant.

Such were his beliefs and his rightness. At meetings and in conversations with friends, he never missed an opportunity to condemn the thieves during communism, comfortably forgetting that he himself was one of them. He was not particularly bothered when judging others, while considering himself impeccable. Okay… But that time had passed, and he knew it. His sole consolation was that his two daughters had found good jobs, were earning well, and did not have to sew nylon pockets.

Perhaps here is the right moment to ask ourselves: what if Donyo's dream had come true? What if he had actually become an economist? Then what would have been his equivalent of a meat processing factory? Maybe a bank? Or a plant? And if so, what form and what kind of products would his mince and sausage be?

WHO CREATES GOOD AND EVIL?

Comrade Chukanov was a well-known teacher in his town. He taught vocational training, but simultaneously held the position of a tutor. Given the status of his persona that was considered "emblematic" for the school, he was also entrusted with a class of which he was the class teacher for four years.

Everyone was aware of Chukanov's authoritarian temper, and none of the pupils manifested much desire to attend his classes. Unfortunately, they had no choice.

Ivan Chukanov had grown up in a small village, a few kilometers away from the town where he moved after the communists came to power. At that time, he had managed to finish evening school, which subsequently opened up the opportunity for him to obtain a teaching diploma and fulfill his childhood dream.

A brief explanatory note to the readers: during the communist era, evening high schools were widely attended by people from the working class, members of the Communist Party who had passed the age for secondary education but lacked the necessary qualifications to get any job. Subsequently, these same evening school graduates were given the opportunity, through a program called the "Worker's Faculty", or "Rabfak" for short, to enroll for higher education, often without an admission exam. The goal was to enhance the qualification of people from the working class, including Communist Party activists, and thus create a kind of working-class elite that would serve as a "pattern to be followed" by the communist educational system.

The actual teaching took place in the buildings of city high schools, although it took place in the evenings, after six o'clock, after the workers had finished their shifts at the factories. For the teachers, this was something like overtime work, and they were able to earn additional fees, which were called "lecture overtime hours" at the time.

The idea was not fundamentally unsound, but sometimes ridiculous situations occurred when high-ranking comrades within the Communist Party had to be examined privately in the principal's office, so as not to be made a laughingstock in front of the ordinary students.

Ivan Chukanov dreamed of being a person whom others depended on, notwithstanding if they were pupils, teachers, or parents – it did not matter. The important thing was to have someone whom he controlled and whose fate he could decide. And the teaching profession presented him with such unlimited opportunities to rule over people. Something that should be mentioned here: no one knew exactly how he had obtained his teaching diploma. His colleagues wondered whether he had graduated from the Rabfak, after the evening school, or had completed some other courses. These were just guesses though, as no one ever dared to comment on it before him. But in any case, it happened – Chukanov became a teacher and took charge of the matters.

What was interesting was where that thirst for power had originated. His fellow villagers remembered Ivan in his adolescent years: a boy rather inconspicuous and showing no such ambition whatsoever. Probably, it had all been instigated by some sort of accident during his military service. There, they nicknamed him The Woodpecker, as his nose was long and crooked, and he really hated his nickname. So much that one day he even dared to shout at his platoon's staff sergeant who had called out to him by his nickname in front of the formation. The sergeant got so angry that without saying a word he punched him straight on the face, knocking him down. That, in turn, caused the violent jeers of the other young soldiers, while Chukanov had been lying on the ground with a bloodied face.

When he had finally stood up, there was no trace of his long, crooked nose. It was now flattened and pulpy. The doctor in the unit concluded that he had never seen such a broken nose, but since it did not obstruct Ivan's breathing, he could go on that way. Word of the unfortunate event reached Chukanov's home village, and when he returned from his service, everyone in the neighborhood began to call him The Woodpecker.

However, all that changed on the day Chukanov became a teacher in the town. It was just then that he felt his time had come. It should be mentioned that during this period, he also joined a volunteer militia unit. The organization of the unit volunteers was a subdivision of the Ministry of Internal Affairs. It had no clear rules or functions, but anyone who would join it received a membership document and became sort of a hybrid officer – neither a uniformed policeman nor an ordinary civilian or a sort of both.

Comrade Chukanov adored the moments when, on the designated evenings he would fasten the band of a volunteer militia member above the elbow of his right arm and, together with his fellow militia members, he would begin patrolling the town garden, chasing students smoking cigarettes. During these actions, he had the opportunity to satisfy his malice by slapping a few solid slaps on the face of a random transgressing student. Thus, Chukanov solidified his reputation as a bad person among colleagues, pupils, and parents.

The school where he taught was an elementary one, up to the eighth grade, and here The Woodpecker was within his element. He never missed an opportunity to impose order and discipline. The principal often received complaints from disgruntled parents about their children being hit or insulted by Chukanov, but he turned a deaf ear to them, as he himself felt intimidated by him.

The reason for this was that Comrade Chukanov, among other things, was a member of the Communist Party. And here, things became entangled and gave him some peace of mind, so to speak, to solve problems in his own way and with impunity, and with the party standing behind him – also to complain, should the principal or a colleague express disagreement with his methods of work.

For the pupils, Ivan Chukanov was the actual embodiment of the devil. During classes, when he got angry, his eyes would instantly begin to shoot sparks, his face would contort with malice, and his flat nose would take on the appearance of a ripe red bell pepper. Immediately afterwards, slaps would follow on the "offending" pupil.

Comrade Chukanov was all but stupid – he knew well whom of the pupils to impose. Usually, his angry gaze rested on the ones whose parents were ordinary workers, while the children of party comrades or his friends were never among the candidates for his fistful re-education. Thus, Chukanov presumed he was building the authority of a strict and principled teacher, and slaps were part of his pedagogical beliefs. But in his essence, The Woodpecker was one big coward in disguise.

Over time, the vocational training classes would prove to be the most difficult and challenging ones for the pupils of the school. Comrade Chukanov employed a unique approach of his own to conduct those classes. His favorite topics were woodworking, steel, and tractors. These three pillars formed the basis of most of the curriculum.

Among them, tractors held the most elect place in The Woodpecker's courses. The reason for this was that his father, a tractor driver on the local farm, had taught him to operate a tractor when he was just a boy, and this, according to The Woodpecker, gave him a significant scientific superiority.

The Communist Party needed loyal people, and Comrade Chukanov had proved himself before the town committee as a principled and disciplined person. That is why, following a decision taken by certain influential party leaders, a separate new building was built in the school yard for practicing and acquiring skills in vocational training. The Woodpecker's dreams had come true – he finally felt himself valued and started living within his own comfort. He was also elected a party secretary of the school, which meant a great power at that time.

But Chukanov had his own deep-seated fears that no one suspected about. According to his teaching schedule, he was required to teach several lessons of electrical engineering per curriculum, a subject that was sort of a *terra incognita* to him. Since childhood, he had spent hours watching electricians at work, merely clicking his tongue, clueless. His worries would intensify even more during the practical classes, as there was an exercise involving assembling and constructing an electrical circuit with the help of a small transformer, a bulb, and a switch.

Once, during one of these classes, Chukanov had made an error while connecting the transformer to the electrical circuit, resulting in a short circuit and a small explosion that filled the classroom with smoke. At that moment, The Woodpecker had quickly jumped and curled into a ball behind the lectern. The students burst into uncontrollable laughter and he could hardly swallow that.

He attempted to remove electrical engineering from the curriculum trying to invoke the party about that issue, but he failed. Then he flipped through an old notebook from when he was about to become a teacher, in which he had jotted down various notes, but he could not find a single line about electrical engineering or physics.

He had decided to get rid of the electrical engineering classes at all costs and eventually managed to persuade the principal to appoint a second teacher who would work two days a month and teach that subject. Thus, he no longer bothered to think about transformers and circuit breakers. After the explosion incident, The

Woodpecker decided to become even more demanding and focused on the lessons about metals, especially his favorite topic – steel. Usually, the vocational training classes would begin with an examination at the blackboard of one or two pupils, after which Chukanov would give a lecture. So once, during the examination, he began to ask a pupil some questions:

'Vesko, tell me now, how many types of steel exist?'

'Three types, comrade,' the pupil chirped.

'Very well, Vesko, very well!' The Woodpecker began to chortle. This classification was an invention of his own. 'They are three, indeed. Now, name them. Which are they?'

'Well, comrade teacher, they are A, B, and C,' Vesko blurted out and fell silent. The classroom erupted in laughter. 'A, B and C…' the entire class was reciting, doubled over in giggles. This, according to Chukanov, was an unacceptable insubordination and without any hesitation he began slapping the "culpable" pupil. Poor Vesko received a total of three slaps: one for the "A", one for the "B", and one for the "C". Red-faced and teary-eyed, the pupil was off home right after the end of the class. His classmates excitedly told other children of the school what had happened, not sparing the mockery and contemptuous epithets for The Woodpecker.

Late that same evening, the principal called Chukanov on the phone. He was annoyed and angry, and warned Chukanov that the boy's father had come to the school in the afternoon, furious, demanding an explanation. He had brought his son and showed off his face severely bruised by the slapping. He threatened that his complaint would not suffice, but there would also be a physical retribution for whoever had committed this abomination.

Bravery was not a particular virtue that Chukanov used to feature. He began to swallow nervously while listening to the principal and started plotting a plan how he could escape the promised payback. He did not sleep a wink all night, and in the morning, he called the school to notify them that he was sick, and taking four days of sick leave he holed up until the tension subsided.

But this was one of the rare occasions when Comrade Chukanov had failed to make a correct assessment where to dispense his personal justice, because usually he did not make mistakes.

In addition to being a vocational training teacher, The Woodpecker also took the post of a class teacher, and this meant that once a week, usually on Mondays, he would also lead the "class teacher's class". It was safe to say that these classes had become his favorite.

During these class teacher's classes, Chukanov could impose his ideas of order and discipline not only in practice but in theory already. Most often, he used this time for the ideological training of the students. He would delve into the theory of communism and, generally, it would always come down to the fact that a pupil should not have a mullet type of longer hair at the back of his neck because this was a toxic sham of the West. And since he could not stand this type of hairstyle, he would often take scissors and a wastebasket and start circling the desks. Those boys who were found to enjoy that particular hairstyle were forced to bend over the wastebasket while Comrade Chukanov was shaping their haircut with the scissors in compliance with his own creed. Everything followed his own rules. The sons of the party comrades would only have three or four millimeters cut off their hair. The others, of course, were trimmed in such a way that holes were cut onto their hair and the next day they would have to come with their heads bald shaved.

Haircut was not the only field in which Chukanov used to find Western influence. What gave him the most trouble were the Charleston pants with straight pockets. The Woodpecker knew that manifestations of sympathies to capitalism must be nipped in the bud, and he had taken this taxing mission dead seriously. Therefore, if during a class teacher's class he detected a pupil wearing Charleston-type trousers (God forbid!) with straight pockets, he would call him at the blackboard and, with well-rehearsed movements, rip his pockets. This really made Chukanov feel complete, although there was whispering among the students about an occasion in which a pair of trousers had turned out to be made of some very strong fabric and Chukanov had ended up grappling with the pockets for a full five minutes, but eventually failed to rip them. Finally, he got infuriated, giving the student a good slap and sending him back to his seat.

So the days and years were going by, and Comrade Chukanov was consolidating his pedagogical technique undisturbed. But one spring morning caught him off guard regarding some unexpected challenges. He was going to the school early to attend a teachers' council that was scheduled to take place an hour and a half before classes. Chukanov had dressed himself to the nines, clean-shaven, ready to philosophize and give out opinions. When he arrived at the school yard, he found his colleagues gathered in front of the entrance of the building talking to each other, waiting for everyone to come. He joined the conversation, but just then a deafening shout caused everyone to freeze in place and turn to the school yard fence:

'Woodpecker! Woodpecker! Hey, Woody!'

Chukanov's face contorted with rage. About thirty meters away, he saw the grinning face of a former student of his, who had stopped with his bicycle in front of the school fence. His name was Gencho, and until two years ago The Woodpecker was his class teacher. Over the years, the young man had taken quite a few slaps from Chukanov, so it did not take long for the latter to realize what it was all about.

'Hey, bonehead!' The Woodpecker started foaming at the mouth as the other teachers watched in disbelief. 'Come here and I'll show you! Who do you call "woodpecker", you moron?'

'Woodpecker!' Gencho kept on shouting at him. 'You're a moron!'

Chukanov was fuming, his nose becoming even more flattened and flushed.

I'm gonna show you, you little brat! Chukanov thought. But just as he was about to approach the cheeky boy, he stopped, stepping back slightly, as if he wanted to duck down. Gencho had taken out a slingshot and was aiming a steel screw at his former class teacher. The other teachers scampered off the entrance. Chukanov had frozen in his place not daring to make a move – he had become a target. Then, Gencho suddenly released the strap of the slingshot and the screw flew away. Chukanov fell face down and heard the screw whizzing past his head and clattering into one of the gutters of the school building. Apparently, the boy only wanted to scare The Woodpecker and make a laughingstock of him.

'Ha-ha-ha… The Woodpecker's got the creeps!' Gencho smirked and rode off, satisfied.

Comrade Chukanov quickly snapped out and jumped to his feet, but his fear prevailed over his malice and he did not dare to undertake any further action. He opted only to pretend he would deal himself with that little rascal:

'Hey, I'm gonna find you, dummy!' The Woodpecker was yelling frantically, trying to bluff that he had taken control of the situation.

Throughout the teachers' council, he did not say a word. He was sitting dead quiet. He knew he had to take revenge to regain his dignity. He was left with his tail tucked between the legs and that made him even more incensed. Finally, the meeting was over, but he was still haunted by thoughts of what had happened and was wandering like a ghost along the corridors.

He perked up only when he entered the vocational training class, where he felt at home. And then, The Woodpecker saw an unexpected opportunity to reclaim his standing. In his absence, a problem had occurred that would require his unconditional intervention. Someone had broken the handle of a hammer from the cabinet's inventory, and according to Chukanov, this was a grave and blatant offense. The resulting situation was among his preferred ones – those when he had to conduct an investigation to find the culprit and eventually to dispense justice. After that humiliating incident in the morning, his authority was at stake and some counteraction had to be initiated. The children were silent, and none of them was willing to betray their comrade, who had unwittingly broken that hammer handle.

'Let the group leader rise up!' The Woodpecker roared. 'Who broke the hammer, comrade group leader?'

Zlatka stood up, her reddened cheeks were revealing her tension as she knew exactly who had broken the hammer, but she did not want to disclose him.

'I do not know, comrade teacher,' she replied.

Chukanov thought for a moment, since the group leader, Zlatka, was the daughter of a high-ranking comrade from the district committee of the party and she was not eligible – so to speak – to slapping. At the same time, he could feel his hands itching, and he thought to himself, *I'll start pushing them one by one until they confess.* And then his voice boomed:

'All right, then… Pupil number one, get into the storeroom.'

Chukanov pointed to the small room behind the blackboard where he kept his inventory of laths and other kinds of timber. Pupil number one, Andrew, got up in terror from his desk and shakily entered the crammed room, but as they say, at the end he gave his classmate's name away without any resistance. The culprit turned out to be the son of a friend and neighbor of The Woodpecker, so the situation was extinguished scot-free. The students quickly collected ten cents each to buy a new hammer and handed them to Chukanov.

I am a pedagogue and I am an excellent one!, The Woodpecker thought proudly. At the end of the class, to enhance his self-confidence and scare the children even more, he said sharply:

'Should I have failed to find out who has broken the hammer, I would have taken you all to the police. And you would have spilled even your guts there.'

Then he gave a smug look around and left the room, victorious.

This is how the days, months and years were going on, until one morning the country woke up and the downfall of communism was announced on the radio. The Communist Party had lost its leading position. The volunteer units of the militia were undone, the party organization in the school, too. Chukanov shrunk into his shell – he sensed his end had come.

After a while, he was retired and people said that he started working as a watchman in his native village, but many did not believe this. No one talked about him anymore. Only some former pupils, when they would meet, years later, reminisced with irony about his teaching methods. Communism had raised people like

Chukanov to power, but with the decisive advent of democracy, each of them got what they actually deserved.

BECOMING A KOMSOMOLETS[10]

The Maurice Thorez[11] Elementary School was built in the beginning of the 1970's in the town of Zlatostrouy. It was not quite clear exactly whose idea it was to name it after Maurice Thorez, but after a memorial corner of the French hero was put up on the second floor, opposite the principal's office, pupils and their parents could read his biography and thus become more familiar with the life of the school's patron. It would not be an exaggeration to say that many local party members struggled to associate the name of that French figure, idealized in our country at that time, with any specific experience. Nevertheless, the Bulgarian people's love for studying meant that the construction of the new school was met with great enthusiasm by the town's folk.

During this period, pupils from the first to the eighth grade experienced a peculiar metamorphosis that had become a hallmark of

---

[10] *Komsomolets*: a member of the Komsomol

[11] *Maurice Thorez (1900 – 1964)*: French politician, leader of French Communist Party (1930 – 1964).

the emerging communist education system. Typically, a pupil in the first grade in school would initially enter a scout organization called "Chavdarche" and wear a blue scarf, while later, in their third grade, he or she would transition to a higher-level scout organization and be called a "Pioneer" and wear a red scarf. Finally, in their upper grades, students were eligible to join the Dimitrov's[12] Communist Youth Union (DCYU) or Komsomol. It was a youth organization affiliated with the Communist Party, which regularly changed its name, and which now simply does not exist anymore. This, by the way, was the natural end of many similar organizations invented during communism that were devoid of any ideas for their further evolution. However, the DCYU once held immense sway over the lives of young people as membership thereof could significantly influence a pupil's future in either direction.

Becoming a Chavdarche and later a Pioneer was obligatory for all pupils, up to seventh grade in school. Admission to the Komsomol, however – although a mass phenomenon and to a certain extent a predetermined path for any student – could prove unattainable for some of the students. Besides the fact that some were never granted membership, others could be subsequently expelled at the discretion of the organization, notwithstanding they

---

[12] Named after Georgi Dimitrov (1882 – 1949). He was a Bulgarian communist politician who served as leader of the Bulgarian Communist Party (1933 – 1949), and the first leader of the Communist People's Republic of Bulgaria (1946 – 1949). He was also General Secretary of the Communist International (1935 – 1943). Source: *Wikipedia*.

had been initially admitted. It was an unofficial rule that a student who was not a Komsomol member could not proceed to university education or get a good job after graduation. But as we said, this was unofficial, concealed somewhere within the government system.

In any school, the principal, the party secretary, and the so-called "company leader" were responsible for shaping the political consciousness of pupils and teachers. As a rule, the company leader would be a woman, whereas it was mandatory for her to be a member of the Communist Party. This person's primary role was to work with the so-called "active members" of the student classes, which invariably included the group leaders and the Komsomol secretaries. Typically, the group leader was one elected among the top pupils of a class, and in case several top pupils were eligible, preference was given to the child of a party official, if any. In short, there was a strict hierarchical system.

The most momentous events for pupils, whether a Chavdarche, a Pioneer, or a member of the Komsomol, occurred during the national holidays. On these occasions, the children would wear white shirts and would tie blue or red scarves around their necks, while the youngest ones wore caps on their little heads with metal lion emblems pinned on as a kind of insignia. All this created an atmosphere of utter joy and excitement, and the entire process took place under the watchful eye of the company leader, who directed the event.

Comrade Svinarska[13] was appointed a company leader at the Maurice Thorez Elementary School. She was thirty-five and had recently graduated from one of the then-modern pre-university schools[14], which implied that following a couple of years of weekend intensive educational courses she had become qualified enough to already perform a kind of psychological dissection of the child's soul.

Her husband, Todor Svinarski[15], had contributed immensely to her sensational career. As a taxi driver, Comrade Svinarski had established solid connections with the town's party activists and managed to intercede with them for his wife's appointment to the newly opened school. Back then, taxis were state-owned and there was a shortage of them.

Todor Svinarski managed to get hold of one of the taxi cars and drove around the town all day, and when there were no customers, he hung out in the parking in front of the only hotel in town. He was extremely satisfied with his job and secretly enjoyed the benefits. Customers would always leave him a tip, and during the rest of the time, nothing could prevent him from popping out and

---

[13] *Svinarska*: In English the name would roughly translate as Mrs. Swinefarmer, which in Bulgarian has a certain negative connotation implying low, rustic origin.

[14] The *pre-university education* differs from the high school one and its closest equivalent is college.

[15] In Bulgarian language, nouns, most pronouns and respectively personal names have a gender: masculine, feminine, or neuter. That's why in the majority of the cases male and female family names differ in their inflections.

doing his personal business, eventually making use of the state property. Often, he even managed to snitch some gas from the taxi for his own car. And he was lucky on several occasions, as in one of the cases he drove a well-known party comrade from the district committee of the party to a meeting in the capital, so he was able to make friends with him. It was that very acquaintance with the local party majesty that helped him secure his wife's appointment to the new school.

Nurtured with the communist ideology, Kina Svinarska took her work seriously, determined to navigate the pupils' development and not to allow any deviation from the right course. In fact, she enjoyed complete freedom in her actions and wielded unlimited power in the school. She liked walking around the building all day, especially during the big daily break between the classes, getting to know the students and sniffing out any potential "leaders" among them with her "psychologist's" intuition. Her pre-university education gave her the self-confidence of a big authority on children's souls, which had caused quite a few faulty conclusions and decisions regarding the pupils. Kina Svinarska would never realize that the human psyche is multi-faceted, multi-layered – versatile if you will – and that it was way beyond her limited capabilities to study it, let alone untangle and interpret it.

But anyway, she had her favorite field of activity where she considered herself an expert – to sort out the seventh-graders into groups for the purposes of their pending admission to the Komsomol – a ritual that the Communist Party created and would sustain until the advent of democracy. When doing this, that small, swarthy woman would take the children's destinies into her own hands and begin without hesitation to distribute them in a first, a second or a third group – according to her personal assessment. This event, seemingly insignificant at the time, was of great importance for the children and used to become a source of tension and anxiety. A note to the reader: the admission to the Komsomol of any student in the course of the first group was a particularly prestigious attestation for him. However, things were not like that at the other end, namely in the third group. There abided those with low grades, bad discipline or simply those who had not earned the trust of Comrade Svinarska.

It is a well-known fact that every adolescent wants to shine in some way, to be distinguished from others. However, in Maurice Thorez Elementary this was seen as a deviation from the righteous path. Certain things were categorized as being "a harmful western influence", although it may now sound absurd. One such misdemeanor was wearing wide-legged Charleston trousers, and the other was the so-called *mullet* men's haircut at the back of the neck.

Such acts of defiance however would hardly escape Comrade Svinarska's watchful eye. She would diligently record the names of any transgressing students and then duly reported them to the principal and the respective class teachers. Inevitably, some kind of punishment was imposed on such a child: from simple admonishment in front of the class, or a notice to the parents written in the pupil's personal grade book, to a formal review of the pupil's conduct at a parent-teacher meeting or a teachers' council. It could also lead to a decrease of the pupil's grade of conduct[16] or, in more extreme cases, even to his transfer to another school. The latter rarely happened, but even the tiniest details anyway were giving Kina grounds to tighten control and occasionally give a lecture on pedagogy to the rest of the teachers. Before that, however, she would always consult the school principal to make sure her opinion never contradicted his; this was important to Svinarska – it was a sort of a proof that she always did what was right. Her colleagues were well aware of that obsequious behavior, and she did not have a single friend among them, whom she would confide in.

But for a moment, let us revert to the Komsomol and its well-structured organization. As I have mentioned earlier, the so-called first group included the class top-graders; on national holidays, they wore sashes across their chests with the words "EXCELLENT STUDENT" written in large red letters. On the public manifestations, often held on different occasions at that time,

---

[16] *Grade of conduct*: In Bulgarian schools during the communist era students were subjected to two kinds of evaluation of their standing at school: the first one were the usual grades given for the level of their educational achievements on the various subjects in the curriculum; the second one were grades given for their general conduct in school and outside it. In case of any infringement – actual or alleged – of the rules and/or the then prevailing general perception of "good and bad", the student's "grade of conduct" could be "lowered" and that could have dire consequences on the student's future opportunities for further education, professional career and even personal life.

they were placed in the front rows of the formation and, as they marched, they passed in front of the tribune where the communist elite from the town's Communist Party committee was lined up. This gave those students exceptional pride and made them feel superior compared to their peers. Understandably, the other children were left in the back rows of the formation, but, frankly, it did not impress them much, because they had got used to it.

The second group of students eligible for admission to the Communist Youth Union were those with very good and good (but not excellent) grades, who were also highly trusted by the party when finishing their seventh grade in school.

The third group, by an unspoken agreement, was the outsiders' group – those were students with poor and average grades, as well as all who, in the opinion of Comrade Kina Svinarska, were deemed undisciplined. But even these rules were not a mandatory criterion, as some unsuspecting child who Mrs. Svinarska simply did not like for some reasons, or whose parents she did not get along with, could end up in this group as well.

After students were admitted to the Komsomol, the procedure continued with their final approval by the leaders of the town's committee of the DCYU. This, so to say, was a kind of exam for which a preliminary line-up of questions, with predefined answers, was distributed in advance, which the future builders of communism just had to memorize in order to respond with the correct answer that the comrades on the committee were already expecting. Although all this may sound a complicated and difficult achievement, in fact, all the students would pass this exam.

Such was the environment that Petar Lyutichev, a fourteen-year-old boy, a graduate of the Maurice Thorez Elementary also grew up in. Pepi, as friends and relatives fondly called him, was a smart, kind boy. In school, he performed more than excellently and he was particularly good at mathematics, notwithstanding math made him feel bored, as did – by the way – any other exact science school subject. On the other hand, he adored literature – it was also his favorite subject. He loved to write essays and analyses of various works, from poetry to novels. He used to spend long hours in the school library, his favorite authors were Karl May and Mayne Reid. His heart throbbed with excitement as he turned with bated breath the pages detailing the exploits and the determination of various brave and steadfast warriors and heroes. But he also had special feelings for poetry, showing an astonishing sense of aesthetics and romance. He even began to write his own poems, which, however, he did not dare to show to a wider audience, except for his younger brother, whom he loved very much.

Apart from being an excellent student, Pepi was also a good friend. Everyone liked him and enjoyed his company, but deep in his soul he allowed just a few to call themselves his friends. He prized loyalty and returned it in kind, sticking by his most devoted friends no matter how big a mischief they would do sometimes.

By then, he was a big fan of most of the popular English rock bands and together with his friends would scour everywhere for new vinyl records or Magnetophon reel-to-reel tapes of their songs and albums. Often, before going to bed, he would play a random track of his preferred ones on his old Magnetophon and dream about being at a concert of some of his favorite bands, getting autographs from the musicians.

At the tender age of fourteen, the concept of freedom was already taking shape in his mind. Rock music was the natural sequel of the adventure novels that used to elate him.

One day, he even took a record to the school and asked the principal to play it over the PA system as a greeting to his classmates. The principal gave him a skeptical look and checked the record but it had no label indicating the artist or song names. Finally, the principal agreed, thinking, *What the heck, it's just a song!*

And so it happened that a song by one of Pepi's favorite English rock bands was blasting over the school PA system. The whole school soon filled with the upbeat music, and students began dancing in their classrooms. However, halfway through the song, the principal, who did not speak a word of English, realized there was something wrong. Infuriated that a pupil had tricked him, he switched off the music. The school fell silent, and everyone was puzzled.

That incident did not escape the attention of Kina Svinarska, who most thoroughly summoned an emergency meeting of the teachers' council, where it was reported about the arbitrary act of an extremely wayward student, who dared to propagate decadent Western music among his peers. This last thing, to be honest, did not worry Pepi much, however more and more questions about freedom of thought and will began to root in his mind, which made him restless.

As time passed, the memory of this event began to fade from his mind, and so the new school year began. Pepi was in the seventh grade and, being an excellent student, he eagerly awaited his well-deserved admission into the first group of candidates for the communist youth union.

One Monday morning, in the class teacher's class, the door opened and Kina Svinarska abruptly showed up, dressed in a black blouse with red collar and red skirt with two large pockets on its sides. She was holding a red file folder with a single sheet of paper sticking out of it.

All the pupils stood up and greeted her in unison. She stood in front of the blackboard and read the names of several students who had been chosen to be among the first ones admitted into the

Komsomol. Peter listened with bated breath and expected to hear his name, but he did not. He was unpleasantly surprised, but he would not let it bother him too much. Although a teenager, he was clearly aware that as a child of ordinary parents – a child of a working-class family, as it was called at the time – his excellent performance at school might not suffice in giving him any advantage.

His father, Galab Lyutichev, was a member of the Communist Party and a former member of the resistance during the war years. After the victory of communism, he had graduated from a high school and then the so-called Higher Party School, but he had never managed to fit into the party nomenclature. On top of that, rumour had it that he had exposed the thefts of a high-ranking Communist Party member, and since then he had been assigned to work in the labor-cooperative farm of a small village near Zlatostrouy. Peter was aware of his father's past and attributed his omittance from the first group of Komsomol candidates to this, but consoled himself with the hope that he would be admitted with the second group.

As the end of the school year was approaching, one day Comrade Svinarska turned up in their classroom again, wearing her invariable black blouse with a carefully ironed red collar and her red skirt with those clumsy, enormous pockets on the sides. She was once again carrying the same red folder, and with a trembling voice, she announced the names of eight more students for the second group to be admitted to the Komsomol. Peter Lyutichev was visibly nervous as he listened to Svinarska reading out the names, and not hearing his own, he felt his stomach churning, and his body fainting. He was disappointed, hurt, and helpless. He – the excellent student – failed to make it into the second group either. Something was wrong, and like most young, free-spirited people witnessing obvious injustice, he decided to demand an explanation. He ran along the corridor, caught up with Svinarska and asked her:

'Comrade Svinarska, for what reason have I not been admitted into that group either?' his voice was trembling with affront.

Kina halted, startled, then laughed guiltily and said:

'Have patience, Peter! There is information you misbehaved in the literature classes, right?'

'Well, how did I behave, comrade company leader?' asked Peter, apparently agitated already, his cheeks reddened. He did not remember doing anything wrongful and he was wondering what Svinarska had come up with.

But she continued confidently, in a didactic tone:

'Well, for instance, you've been laughing, you've been questioning your grades, and that is not an attitude expected from a future komsomolets. To put it simply, you're not disciplined enough. If I had the authority, I'd have you kicked out. I still remember how you got the principal to play that decadent song.'

Svinarska was getting infuriated. She did not like insubordinate people, especially those whose opinion differed from her own as a company leader of the school. The pedagogical approach she used to apply in those occasions aimed to break the will of such rebels. She turned to leave but halted again and hissed viciously, very quietly, just for him:

'Should you go on this way there's gonna be no Komsomol for you, I guarantee!'

And she walked away, clearly satisfied that she had given a good lesson to a fourteen-year-old boy who was looking stunned, confused, and not knowing what to say.

Throughout the summer Peter was gloomy because all his friends had been admitted to the Komsomol, and he had not. That thought was devastating to him. He started avoiding his friends, rather spending his time at home, locked in his room.

He felt wronged and humiliated. He had a perception for a great injustice happening to him, realizing he was powerless to fight back or change anything. He was asking himself numerous questions, seeking fault in himself. Indeed, he was clueless about what the inside of this organization, they called "the Komsomol", was like; he did not know anything about its rules or ideology. He was just a fourteen-year-old child whose soul was deeply wounded.

His bad mood worried his parents. His father, Galab Lyutichev, tried to talk to him and calm him down, but he failed to really get to the bottom of his son's feelings. Nevertheless, Galab was a brave and resolute man; he knew how to cope in such a situation and did not waste time. As a party member and a former resistance activist, he still had access to the Communist Party district committee and turned to the members of the party bureau for help.

The first secretary of the town committee did not like Comrade Svinarska and had long been waiting for a chance to put her in her place. He considered her a rather mediocre woman anyway, and now he was just informed that, on top of everything else, Kina was not capable of working with the children of the party elite.

A few days after Galab Lyutichev's visit to the first secretary, Svinarska was summoned to appear at the town party committee. The whole night before the meeting, she could not get asleep and wondered what she had done wrong for being called to a meeting from which she could not expect anything good to come out. Her husband made several calls trying to find out what was going on, but all was in vain.

From early in the morning, Svinarska was waiting in front of the room of the first secretary of the party, and when she finally was entered, he began angrily, before she had even closed the door:

'Svinarska, do you know that Peter Lyutichev is the son of one of our comrades who was a member of the resistance?' And without waiting for an answer from the stunned Kina, he continued even more fiercely: 'And do you know that if his father files a complaint to the district party committee, I'm out of here?' He paused for a moment, swallowed, and without taking his eyes off her, went on: 'But before that, *you* are going to be out, and your husband will no longer drive a taxi and you will be growing tomatoes in your native village! Do you realize that? You don't know our people, comrade company leader! You don't know!'

The whole tirade was apparently over, there was silence and Kina hurried to answer without thinking much because she understood how serious the situation was. As for her being fired or returning to the village – she would rather die.

'I'm going to fix all that, comrade secretary!' Her voice trembled. 'Forgive me, I don't know how I could have made this terrible mistake,' she began reproaching herself, 'how I missed that his father was from the resistance… But this will not happen again, I can assure you! Give me a chance and I'll fix everything!' she whimpered at the end.

The First Secretary did not even glance at her. He had already solved the problem, and Kina would know her place now. He called his secretary, and she came in to escort Svinarska out, who was even more confused because she still was not quite sure: was she going to keep her job or she had been fired; would she be expelled from the party, or just reprimanded by her comrades at a meeting. And about Peter Lyutichev and his Komsomol membership – Kina couldn't care less now.

She returned to the school and wandered around the teachers' room, but it seemed like no one was in the course of her issues. A little later, the principal appeared at the door and nodded for her to follow him. As they stepped out into the hallway, he told her sternly:

'Svinarska, no more screw-ups, right!'

And she sighed in relief – apparently, there would be no consequences for her.

At the beginning of the eighth grade, the last eight students from Pepi's class were admitted to the Komsomol. Svinarska was also attending the ceremony for their approval by the city committee and, without any introduction, she started praising Peter. The Komsomol secretary listened to her and not able to contain his curiosity he asked:

'We're accepting him into the Komsomol just with a third group... Although he's been an excellent student, right? Why?'

Kina leaned towards the secretary and explained in a fawning tone:

'It's my mistake, Comrade Komsomol Secretary. Issues arise when one's working with so many people, but this won't ever happen again.

Subsequently, everything went according to the procedure. They took all the newly admitted Komsomol members by bus to a neighboring village, where a well-known member from the anti-fascist resistance was born, and handed them their Komsomol membership cards. Peter Lyutichev watched the pompous ceremony and wondered if that resistance member, killed in the years of the war, had once imagined that a day would come when such an organization like the Komsomol would exist.

Svinarska had clearly learned her lesson, as Peter was the first one to receive his card. This caused whispers and laughter among his friends, as they knew what had happened to Kina at the town party committee.

Pepi was in a good mood, but not because he was becoming a komsomolets. The reason was much more existential—an injustice had been righted. Later, as a university student, he witnessed something that convinced him of the meaninglessness of all these attributes. One day, the Komsomol secretary of his university course fell drunk from the bridge on the coastal boulevard into the sea, holding in his hand the briefcase in which he used to keep his colleagues' Komsomol membership cards. The briefcase sank, and with it, all the cards. Thus, the Komsomol organization was left without an archive, but no one said a word about it, and no one cared anyway.

Time passed and the world turned upside down, democracy triumphed in the country, and there were neither Komsomol nor Komsomol membership cards. Only the sadness of a wounded child's heart remained in Peter for a lifetime. *Children are so far from politics – they just love to play and have fun. They have their hearts pristine and we, adults, must respect them!*, Peter often thought.

Now people are free and no one remembers the Komsomol or the admission procedure. Kina Svinarska retired and returned to live in her village. Peter Lyutichev finished his higher education and took a job in Germany.

And the Maurice Thorez Elementary school was renamed to Renaissance Elementary.

THE PASSIONAL OF LITKO POPOV

Litko Popov was a man in his fifties. Of average height and a slender build, he had dark eyes and black hair that was starting to gray. When viewed from behind by someone taller, a bald spot was visible at the crown of his head. Always clean-shaven, he was perpetually spritzed with Denim cologne. [Note: Denim cologne was already available in Bulgarian stores in the 1980s.] Litko had an energetic and brisk gait, a result of his profession.

Popeto, as everyone used to call him, was a waiter, and so was his wife. They had two daughters, already married, so the spouses were living alone. They had a large, four-room apartment on the third floor. Their building had only one entrance, and there were three apartments on each floor. It was built of brick, which was highly valued at the time of Communism when panel construction was dominant but rather unfavoured by most people.

His car was a white Lada, and unlike most people, Litko had not had to wait a decade to buy it. He managed to get ahead in the queue by paying someone off under the table – a common practice back then. He needed the car for his commute to work. Both he and his wife worked at the restaurant of a prestigious hotel in the Stardust complex, which was about twenty kilometers from their home. The tourist season typically began in early April and lasted until the end of October. In April, they usually started cleaning the kitchen and the restaurant, preparing for the high season, even though there were always guests from the very first days of the month.

During the winters Popeto was not working. He and his wife would rest, recharging for the next summer. And he had a good reason for that, because in addition to the money they earned during the summer, they received a monthly rent for the two rooms that his mother was letting out to students. Aunt Nelly, as the students called her, was a sociable and cheerful woman, well-known for her shrewdness. She was skilled at making friends quickly when it was to her advantage. She was practical and insisted on strict rent payments. She had been widowed at a young age and had raised her son on her own. In her youth, she had done some rather shady things that she stubbornly hid from people. After her husband's demise, she had started engaging in the illegal trade of small gold jewelry – chains, rings, and the like – something unthinkable in an exemplary communist state. This had certain consequences – after the police had caught her, she had spent about two years in prison.

Her time in the slammer had a sobering, even ennobling effect on Nelly, so much that after serving her sentence, she had become a fervent activist of the Fatherland Front, one of the mass public organizations during the communist era.

However, all this was just "minor details" from the dark side of her biography, which would sometimes surface in her mind when reminiscing about that time.

Nelly had played a major role in shaping Popeto's personality. Despite the fact that his late father was a respected engineer, her life experiences had convinced her that university education was not quite a useful one. Therefore, she directed Popeto towards the profession of a waiter after he graduated from high school.

'Litko,' she would say, 'I'm going to send you to your Uncle Vesko, who works as a waiter. Learn the trade. All you have to do is watch and listen. Be smart!'

And Popeto followed his mother's advice – she was after all regarded as a complete erudite among their town's community at that time – and he began working as a waiter. However he would never regret it, because the job had certain advantages. For example, if someone worked hard and diligently during the summer, he could conveniently take the winter off. And if they were eager enough, nothing stopped them from going to one of the winter resorts in the country and working there until the summer season.

The career of Popeto was on the rise. In his very first summer, he bought three color TVs with just his tips and put one in each room. The following year, he got the Lada, and so, step by step, he was setting up his life. He spent nearly a decade at the restaurant where he started his career. During that time, he got married, managed to buy his own home, and fully furnished it. After his daughters got married, Popeto could now focus solely on making money.

After a while, an old acquaintance of his, also a waiter, sought him out to tell him that a new hotel was opening the following summer, again in the Stardust complex.

'This new hotel is going to be a massive one, pal,' his friend was persuading him. 'A huge restaurant; and they're expecting foreign tourists only. So, there's gonna be a lot of money to be made. I can talk to the maître d'hôtel for you if you're interested.'

Popeto would not rush to answer. He decided to think it over for a few days. It was true that he made good money in tips at the restaurant where he worked, but it was unlikely that it would be enough for anything more than buying a second Lada or renovating his mother's house. 'And my two daughters are already married,' he reasoned, 'now that grandchildren will be coming up, I would hardly cope.'

And so, the following summer, Popeto ended up at the newly built Diamond and Gold Hotel.

The building was impressive, ten stories tall and right next to the beach. There was a large swimming pool in the courtyard, and the hotel offered modern amenities for that time, including a hair salon, physiotherapy treatments such as therapeutic baths and ionic vaporization, and many more.

The restaurant where Popeto worked was called The Big Walnuts. It was a three-storey establishment with an outdoor area featuring a garden of walnut trees. However, when it rained, the tables in the garden, out in the open, became unusable.

Since the hotel was new, and the investment was made by the state, and it was a substantial one, the management had decided that no "misfits" would be tolerated. Therefore, the staff was carefully selected. Everyone was either an acquaintance of someone in the management, with whom they had worked together before, or had been recommended by a friend of one of the managers. In short, everything was made by the book. This was how Popeto managed to get a job at the restaurant, with the reputation of a long-time waiter who knew all the ins and outs of the trade.

From its very first year, the hotel operated primarily on what is now called "all-inclusive" basis. The guests who stayed there were actually almost exclusively foreigners, so their entire stay, including the meals, was prepaid before their arrival. In the morning, breakfast in the restaurant would continue until ten or eleven o'clock, after which the dining would seamlessly transition into lunch. However, the prepaid part would end with the dinner.

The big profits were coming in the evenings, after eight o'clock, when the restaurant started operating as a pay-per-visit establishment, and consequently, the tips started rolling in. Numerous customers were attracted by the elegant atmosphere, the unique menu, and the nightly entertainment program, which featured only national pop stars, and the host was a well-known comedian from the capital.

All these details were important when determining how the staff would be scheduled for shifts. Typically, the shift that served breakfast and lunch was given to the younger and less experienced waiters, those who were still considered "green". It was their honor to carry the trays and run up and down the stairs of the three-storey building without any chance of receiving a tip. The only perk for them was that they could sneak in a friend or family member to eat for free. Everyone was aware of this practice; however it was not a problem, as food was abundant at the time, and even higher-ups like the maître d'hôtel and other supervisors in the hotel often took advantage of it.

The big money would be made in the evenings. That was the time of the "sharks", or in other words, the "old dogs" – the waiters who were seasoned veterans in the industry. Popeto, having carried trays for about ten years, was one of them and had become even more cunning. But the key figure in the whole operation was the maître d'hôtel, the person who assigned the staff and was responsible for the entire restaurant. Everything went through him – from the menu and table assignments to the waiters' schedules.

The "maître" himself had worked as a regular waiter for many years, so besides being a direct supervisor, he also acted as a spiritual mentor to his subordinates. Everyone could get valuable advice from him on how to earn a bigger tip, how to get familiar with customers, and even how to overcharge a bill. Overall, the waiter's profession was elevated to a kind of highly specialized activity. It was important for a waiter to "feel" the customer, to assess, for example, when the customer was a bit tipsy or when he was not attentive enough, so that the waiter could add a vodka or a whiskey or two to the bill, and sometimes even charge him in dollars or Deutsche marks. These were the seconds when the waiter suddenly turned into a circus magician, or rather, a tightrope walker, trying to balance without falling down. And that last part was important because sometimes gaffes were made, resulting in scandals over the overcharged bills. The dining room manager did not approve these, and whoever made a mistake would work only in the mornings for a long time, setting up the tables, without being allowed to appear in the evenings. Popeto, however, did not make mistakes. He "felt" the customer and knew what he was doing.

So, a kind of private business had sprung up within the state-owned restaurant and it was thriving. Against this backdrop, the maître d'hôtel was left with only his regular salary and, in theory at least, was not entitled to any tips. Commanding twenty waiters, each making extra money, was a frustrating reality. So, the Maître had pondered for quite a while on how to solve that problem and finally devised the following scheme: every evening, around ten fifty, he would appear in the restaurant wearing a velvet blazer. The blazer was blue, with two outer pockets. After walking around the tables to ensure that everything was running smoothly, the Maître would eventually go to the kitchen, where he would take off his blazer and hang it on a wooden hanger, then leave elsewhere. During this time, the waiters on duty, shuttling between the kitchen and the dining room, would discreetly slip money into the blazer pockets, five or ten leva each, depending on how much they had made in tips. No exceptions were made, as everyone knew what the blue blazer signified.

At eleven thirty, the maître d'hôtel would reappear from somewhere and put his blazer back on. Then he would put on his hat and leave. At home, he would take the money out of the pockets and start counting before falling asleep. After all, the Maître was human too, and he had a family that depended on him. But the outcome would be just evident in the mornings. If the shifts table remained unchanged, it meant the Maître was satisfied with the money they had left him. However, if he thought the money was too little, there would be an immediate "rotation", and as a result the morning shift of waiters would become the evening shift and vice versa.

Popeto knew all of these rules and would usually pass by each waiter just before eleven o'clock to prevent any possible blunders. That was how he had succeeded in working mostly the evening shifts for ten years. During this time, Litko eagerly watched the blue blazer every night. It had become a symbol of prosperity and success for him. Very often at night, before falling asleep, he imagined himself one day appearing with a blue velvet blazer and leaving it on the hanger in front of the kitchen. He had even dreamed about it once, but for now, it remained just an aspiration.

So, year after year, season after season, night after night, the cycle continued without the maître d'hôtel ever changing his blazer. He wore it for ten years, every night, although only for about half an hour, but that was just enough to leave a lasting impression on Popeto's mind.

In the eleventh year, changes came. The Maître was promoted to oversee the entire hotel. This stirred up a lot of excitement among the waiters. Everyone knew that one of them would eventually wear the blue blazer, and they all rubbed their hands together secretly, hoping to get their hands on that position. Eventually, luck was on Popeto's side, and he became the new boss. The day after, the former Maître summoned him to his new office and handed him the blue blazer.

Nevertheless, the old Maître forgot neither his former subordinates nor the ten years of financial comfort and peace that these people had provided for him. He silently gave his blessing for the "blue blazer tradition" to continue. And indeed, Popeto not only continued it but made no changes to the system that the Maître had built. There was no reason to do so anyway. The past had shown that the scheme was working flawlessly.

Popeto had entered a new phase of his life and was enjoying his new position. He took pleasure in checking that the restaurant's guests were well-served, played the role of a lackey to various inspecting party and administrative leaders, and every evening at ten fifty, he would hang the blue blazer on the hanger in front of the kitchen. He had mastered the rules of the game from his spiritual mentor, the Maître. His income had also increased, allowing him to take trips abroad during the winters, and he began saving money for his grandchildren as well.

Two years had passed since Popeto had become the dining room maître. Although the system was working flawlessly, he somehow felt a desire, whether it was due to his ego or some greed, to leave his mark on the restaurant's history. So, he ordered a special velvet fabric from abroad, again in blue, to have his own bespoke blazer. He had paid a lot of money for the fabric and when he went to the tailor, he gave him special instructions:

'When sewing the blazer, make sure it has larger pockets!'

And so it was done. The blazer was tailored with large outer pockets.

Now they'll be able to stuff in more money, Popeto thought fondly as the new summer season began.

Popeto had a wonderful season at the restaurant and collected a lot of money, but that same year, changes came to the country. November came and communism fell. The following year, the hotel was privatized and sold, and Popeto was the first to be fired. It was a hard blow on him, one he could not comprehend. He had not expected such a turn of events. He had aspired to the blue blazer for so long, and now suddenly everything had lost its meaning. In his anger, he decided to throw the blazer in the trash, but before that, he searched the pockets and found five crumpled levas.

What an irony…, Popeto chuckled bitterly to himself. He pocketed the five leva and threw the blue blazer away.

Some time later, he ran into his old friend, the Maître, on the street. The other man grinned from ear to ear:

'Hey, Popeto, how are you doing?'

'So-so,' replied Popeto. 'And you, Maître, how are things going for you? How are we both going to manage from now on? Things have changed…'

'Popeto, I couldn't care less about it, my boy,' the Maître replied loudly. 'I have four apartments, and I'm gonna rent them out. You know – there are enough students for all of us. I've set aside some money and I'm going to retire,' he laughed smugly.

Popeto also started laughing:

'I have a couple of apartments too, so I think I'll become a landlord as well. Maybe fate has made us similar in that way. After all, you've always been the example in life for me.'

'That's right, Popeto! It's a pity that we can't do anything else besides what we used to do at the Walnuts. Now I have grandchildren, and I'm urging them to study and get qualified so that they can succeed.'

'You're right, Maître,' Popeto replied thoughtfully, 'our time has passed.'

'But we lived well, Popeto! It's time to rest,' the Maître laughed again.

They parted with a hug. The era of communism was over. Now they were both peacefully aging in the seaside city. As the thinker said, "Panta rhei." Every era produces its own people and professions, every era produces its own heroes, workers, and "sharks".

TWO COMRADES

They were both born in the early 1960s in a small provincial town during the height of real communism. They lived in the same neighborhood. Their childhood passed peacefully and buoyantly, filled with endless games and fun in the playground between the apartment blocks. The communist state had set itself the goal of building recreational areas for all young people, but what was most remarkable about these so-called *children's playgrounds* was that strong friendships were formed there from a very young age and these would last a lifetime.

And that was the case with both our characters as well. One of them was named Jean, an intelligent and gentle boy with a particular sense of humor. He was adored by his neighborhood friends and had rightfully earned the reputation of a loyal companion who would never betray his crew, no matter what mischief they had got up to.

The other one was called Momchil, but everyone called him Memo, even his mother. He possessed a cheerful nature and usually pertained to that part of the posse that used to get into the most of the hassle. Whenever there was a "mishap" in the playground or around the apartment blocks, Memo was always the first suspect and alleged instigator. So, from his very young years, he had a reputation as someone who always found a way to get into trouble.

Speaking about that entire microenvironment, let us also recall the general layout of neighborhoods at the time, or more specifically, the life and relationships between people living therein.

At that time, Communist Party leaders loved to introduce "innovations" in construction and architecture that were meant to symbolize the eternal search for the path to prosperity and perfection in the newly emerging society.

For this reason, a policy of expropriating property and clearing land for the construction of new brick and panel block apartments began in the small provincial town. These properties, previously privately owned, were most often houses that, in most cases, needed major renovations, and their owners usually did not have the necessary funds for such. On the face of it, the party's actions looked timely and reasonable.

However, it was questionable whether the penchant to newly constructed apartment blocks was the most logical move. It was hardly a good idea to force a family that had spent their entire lives in their own house, with a yard and a garden, to move into a fourth-floor apartment in a panel block with a design from the post-World War II period.

But our country, which was largely agrarian at that time, needed to "modernize" and "put an end to its capitalist past", or at least that was the ambition of the new rulers.

Between the newly constructed buildings, there were gardens where children played from dawn till dusk. Later, they were called playgrounds and were equipped with slides and climbing frames, and in some places with football pitches or other sports facilities.

The small provincial town was no exception. The quietness there was just enviable, with incidents or criminal offenses being quite uncommon. There were almost no thefts, and most people would not even lock their front doors. Anyway, the People's Militia was the one keeping the public order.

People used to furnish their new homes in a largely uniform way. The living room invariably featured what was known as a "living room set", which consisted of a sofa with two armchairs and two stools, a small coffee table, and invariably two or three bookcases. The other rooms were a dining room and a bedroom, not counting the kitchen and bathroom.

Here, it is worth paying special attention to perhaps the most iconic element of homes in a socialist apartment block: the cellar.

It was like a small room located under the ground floor where the owners could store their home clutter. Each apartment had a separate cellar, marked with the corresponding number of the apartment. In the autumn, most men used these spaces to store their homemade wine and rakia. The alcohol, accordingly, turned the cellars into important centres of social life. These small underground rooms offered husbands a precious opportunity to steal a moment of freedom and, under the pretext of going downstairs to do some work, get drunk there with friends. It was a common practice to drink wine from jars in the cellar and snack on homemade sausages, which were traditionally hung on long poles and left to dry therein. It was not an exception for a real hero to fully drain his wine barrels too early, in the middle of the winter, and then he would have to wander around town trying to somehow get an additional supply of alcohol, an occasion that, in turn, would become the source of numerous jokes among his neighbors. The wives did not like their husbands lingering in the cellars for too long and sometimes they had to personally go downstairs and collect their drunken spouses.

Back then, what was bad was not that people drank too much; because – let us be honest – anyone has done it, anyway. The real problem was that when a person would let their hair down and drink with friends, their tongue tended to loosen up and they became more talkative. And often, in those drinking circles, there would be an informant, essentially a kind of agent of the secret services. Such a person's job usually involved writing regular reports to the political police, always slandering someone close to him. Often, that particular "someone" could always turn out to be an unsuspecting bloke who had just gotten drunk with friends in the cellar the night before.

But cellars were not solely male domains. In the autumn, the housewives would also go down there to prepare casks of sauerkraut for the winter, a tradition that, incidentally, is still observed nowadays. In the summer, the children would come down, tired from incessant play, to drink water, play cards, and escape the day heat. So, to sum it up, we can safely conclude that such a social and domestic arrangement was rather similar throughout most of the buildings and neighborhoods, especially in the newly built apartment blocks.

The simple truth was that people back then were equally poor and equally rich. If any social stratification was apparent at the time, it originated mainly by the higher echelons of the Communist Party activists, which did not exist in small towns. Instead, there was another, self-made caste of butchers, grocery store clerks, bartenders, and waiters who, at that time, were the people who used to earn more compared to the general public. That was when the expression "to have the cash register hit you in the stomach" came up, meaning to work in a store and have access to the money that, in those days, was kept in the drawer under the counter. There was always some kind of "surplus" in commerce, and so these people had more money to spend.

This latter fact often necessitated inspections by regulatory authorities to ensure the accuracy of weighing scales and other such equipment, as the embezzlement did not involve actual theft from the cash register. For instance, there was a common practice of the groceries to leave cheese to soak in water before selling it, which would increase its water content and weight respectively, and – when sold – this would result in additional "surplus" which, in turn, meant profit for the grocer.

On one occasion, at one of those drinking parties in the cellars, a shopkeeper was telling a story about how he had dug a hole in the basement and hidden five thousand levs, coming from such "surpluses", in glass jars, since there was no way to deposit them into the bank. However, because he did not want the banknotes to be ruined by the damp, he first filled the jars with rice, because he had heard that this would help them stay dry and preserve longer. Later, people like him would exchange these hidden levs for American dollars, which they used to buy things on "the black market". So, that whole process would undergo an evolution of its own.

But let us come back to Jean and Memo. The two friends were children of ordinary office workers, and their parents' salaries were roughly equal. Consequently, whatever one of them had, the other would have as well. For example, if the store sold projectors, both of them had one; if the clothing store released kids' jeans, each of them got a pair from their parents. However jeans like Levi's, Super Rifle, or other Western brands were not available in our stores at the time. This, let us call it material equality, would contribute to the building of an honest and sincere friendship between the two boys, which both of them managed to maintain throughout their lives.

Nevertheless, there had to be some difference in these boys' lives, and in this case, it was their performance in school. There was no equality in school grades, and everyone got what he deserved, but this did not encumber their friendship in any way as envy was a feeling they were not aware of.

The first actual parting of the two happened during their military service. And regarding the service, both of them fully adhered to the then-existing tradition of the "sent-off" of the future soldier. Essentially, the "sent-off" was an alcohol-fueled party that was organized for every young man who was about to go into the military, since in those years, the draft was mandatory. The meaning of this feast to the recruit himself would be somehow ambiguous, least to say – after all, he was about to serve in the army for a whole two or three years. His relatives and friends however looked forward to the date of the event, exploiting that opportunity in order to get drunk beyond belief.

Eventually, both Jean and Memo completed their military service and went their separate ways. Jean went to study engineering in the town of X, while Memo went to another district town to finish his technical school through a part-time course. They were young men now, not the schoolboys they used to be. Their lives were following their natural course and were changing, while at the same time, changes were occurring both within the country and throughout the world. But even though they were, like everyone else, subject to the evolution of time, it did not make them lose their mindset and their typical behaviour that used to unite them as persons and, most importantly, as friends.

One winter, in the early 1980s, Jean found himself back in his hometown. He had returned from X to study in peace for the upcoming exam session in the university, which seemingly would be incredibly difficult this time. In addition to his regular exams, he had to prepare and defend his thesis before a committee. He was excited because he was just a few months away from the moment when he would receive his degree in civil engineering and finally start his career.

Right around that time, as if out of nowhere, an unexpected social upheaval erupted within the country. The communist government had taken a decision to change the names of the local population of Turkish ethnic origin[17], replacing their typical Turkish names with Bulgarian ones. This unleashed a wave of unrest and riots in certain regions of the country. In the first days of the escalating tension, Jean followed the development of the events but continued to diligently prepare for his upcoming exams. He tried not to get distracted, as he did not have much time left to prepare.

But just about a week after the events had begun his landlady from city X called to tell him that the district military authorities were looking for him to call him in as a military reservist. Jean listened attentively to the excited female voice on the other end of the line, his heart pounding.

'But how?' the future engineer stammered in bewilderment. 'I'm a university student! In a few months, I'm gonna be an engineer.'

He just could not utter a word. He hung up the phone and strode down the hallway toward his room when his mother appeared from the living room.

'Why are you so pale?' the dignified lady asked worriedly.

'Mom, it's all over. That was it!'

---

[17] Being once a part of the Ottoman Empire, Bulgaria still features a large Turkish ethnic minority.

'What's over, my boy?' Her lips trembled as if she were about to cry.

'They're drafting me. Probably mobilizing me because of all that turmoil.'

At that moment, the older woman's emotions did a complete 180 degree turn. Her readiness to cry was replaced by a desire to slap her son, but she did not. Instead, she began to lecture:

'Of course, they're going to mobilize you. Can't you see what's going on out there?'

'Yes, but I'm a student, Mom,' Jean interrupted her sarcastically. 'I'm going to be a graduate, even more importantly, a specialist. I'm going to work with my mind, not with some weapons.'

'Don't make me spank you at your age,' the old woman snapped. 'Get ready, because they mean business this time.'

'I *am* getting ready, and it's *me* they're mobilizing me, not you, right?' Jean grumbled sourly and slammed the door of his room.

On one thing he had agreed with his mother – the situation was indeed serious. He was supposed to travel the next day and, as he found out from the information bureau at the station, the train to X had been canceled. Jean did not have a car, and he had never bothered to get a driver's license. Still, he did not have to ponder long about what to do. He called his friend Memo and they agreed to travel early the next morning in Memo's Moskvich so they could cross the Balkan Mountains while it was still daylight.

The night proved to be unbearably long for Jean. He could not fall asleep and lamented his bad luck. He felt wronged and thought that someone else should go in his place. *We'll see how all those big talkers feel if anything happens to me. They'll have to live with that...*, he thought, and a bitter smile twisted his face. Around five in the morning, he got dressed, grabbed his bag of clothes, and went outside to wait for Memo.

Outside, darkness was wafting, mingled with a thick, impenetrable fog. It was very cold; the temperature had probably dropped to minus fourteen or fifteen degrees. For the past few days, it had been snowing endlessly, and a thick snowy blanket had covered the earth. To make matters worse, the roads were icy, making transportation even more difficult. 'We'll see how all this is gonna end,' Jean muttered grimly as he lit a cigarette.

Three or four minutes passed, and two faint lights flickered in the distance, barely piercing the heavy fog. *It's Memo*, Jean thought and threw his cigarette onto the snow. He grabbed his bag and waited for the slowly approaching car. But something was wrong. As the car drew closer, a very distinctive, sputtering sound began to emanate from it. Jean squinted, blinded by the headlights, and concluded that perhaps someone had cast a spell on him. A classic East German Trabant[18] pulled up beside him, and inside, at the driver's seat, the face of Memo was grinning, who began cranking the handle to lower the window.

'Good morning,' he was giggling, his mustache seeming to have frozen from the cold. 'Your car is waiting for you, Comrade Engineer.'

'You call that a car? We won't even make it there by the day after tomorrow, and that's only in case the wind fails to blow us into a ditch.'

'Stop complaining so early in the morning, the car's fine,' Memo continued to chuckle. 'The Moskvich's battery died last night. But later we were hanging out in Uncle Vesko's cellar, and he told me I can take his Trabant. He even filled a jug of wine especially for us.'

'You've drunk up all your wine again?' Jean asked rhetorically, as he placed his luggage in the back seat next to the woven jug.

'I ran out of it a month ago, but the brandy in that bottle is mine, and Aunt Stanka gave me some bacon and sausage for the road.'

---

[18] *Trabant* is a series of small cars produced from 1957 until 1991 by former East German car manufacturer VEB Sachsenring Automobilwerke Zwickau. It became emblematic of the Communist Era in Eastern Europe for its old-fashioned design (although it was considered a bit funny) and low quality.

They set off, and Jean gradually began to calm down as his friend explained that, as a rule, before mobilizing someone, they could release them from the reserve service if they had a good reason. According to Memo, when Jean would get there, he should explain that he was a student and that he was just about to graduate. That way, there would be no reason to draft him, and should he also mention he was going to be a civil engineer, then getting out of the draft would be a done deal. After these comforting words, Jean felt relieved and began to regain his usual cheerful mood.

As expected, the journey was tough and long. It might be just bad luck that the winter was a record cold one, and throughout that day the weather was overcast and windy. The road they had chosen followed the coastline of the Black Sea, but ran about thirty to forty kilometers inland. Even so, they could feel the usual sea breeze - icy and humid at this time of year. The cold had frozen the road so much that in some places the surface was like a skating rink, and the snowdrifts covered the shoulder of the road in most sections, making it very difficult to control the car at times.

Despite the harsh conditions outside, the inside of the car was warm and cozy. Only someone who drove a Trabant knows what that experience was like. The car was an icon of the communist bloc. It was assembled in East Germany and was some sort of "a people's car". It weighed just over half a ton and was made of duroplast, but it was a common joke that it was actually made of cardboard. Some claimed it was not cardboard, but plastic. Its engine was a two-stroke model, and so the sound it made was unmistakable. On the road, it had the looks of a soapbox and in most cases, it shook quite a bit. In the blizzard that was raging during our two characters' journey, it barely managed to stay on the road and to avoid flying off a mountain cliff.

The unforgiving weather did not bother the two friends at all. They were chain-smoking during the entire trip. Memo had brought a few boxes of Marlboros, and the car was filled with an aromatic tobacco smoke. Music was blaring from the radio, and they were animatedly sharing those typical guy stories about women, lovers, and flirtations, their loud laughter filling the car. At one point, they noticed they had not seen a single car on the road yet, and the blizzard seemed to have no intention of letting up. For some reason, this only cheered them up even more, and they decided to drink some wine.

The most challenging part of their journey was still ahead: the crossing of the Balkan Mountain in a Trabant. They had not eaten yet and were starting to get hungry. They pulled the car over under an overpass for some shelter. Memo took out some of Aunt Stanka's bacon, while Jean was tearing big chunks of bread off a loaf. They filled their bellies and had a sip of Uncle Vesko's homemade red wine. It was dry and good, helping them to warm up and gain more courage. And they needed that courage, as they still had not even covered half the distance. They had just over two hundred kilometers left to reach X. The snow had stopped, but the wind was still raging. Before they set off again, Memo took a can of gasoline from the trunk and filled up the tank. Now they were ready.

He drove off to the Balkan Mountain pass. The music continued to play, but they were both silent now. Memo had to concentrate on driving and watch the road. This pause gave Jean a chance to think. He rested his head against the window and gazed at the landscape. Everything around was covered in white. Villages flashed by one after the other. They crossed a bridge over a frozen river. *You wouldn't imagine with all this snow*, Jean pondered, *but in the summer it is so beautiful, with so many flowers and greenery…*

Suddenly, he remembered the purpose of their journey. His stomach churned, and a shiver ran down his spine, spreading throughout his entire body. He was going to be drafted! Or more likely, he would be mobilized! *They're gonna draft me anyway*, Jean bitterly swallowed. *There's no way out of it. And my exam is pending. They wouldn't give a damn about it. No respect for education. And I believed studying would bail me out…* This dark thought was unbearable. He took a swig from the jug of wine and then passed it to Memo, who would never turn down a good drink. After a minute or two, Jean's mind cleared, and there was no trace of his gloomy mood. *I guess this is the way*, he grinned to himself.

Alcohol will prevail over injustice. And the two friends just picked up on their interrupted conversation about women.

After a while, they spotted a barrier in the distance. As they got closer, they realized it was a military checkpoint. Jean immediately recognized them as reservists, also mobilized due to the recent events in the country. They were unkempt and bearded, and most of their clothes did not fit.

One of the reservists ambled towards the car, staggering slightly, with a cigarette dangling from his lips. He introduced himself as a sergeant.

'Passports for inspection!'

Jean and Memo showed their passports. The sergeant, apparently a bit tipsy, grinned at them and leaning into the car window, asked, 'Are you guys crazy or something? Where are you going in this winter and at this very moment?'

They explained where they were headed and got their passports back. Before parting ways, they left him the bottle of rakia.

The Trabant chugged slowly, at about forty to fifty kilometers per hour, on the snowy mountain road. Somewhere in the early afternoon, they stopped again in a relatively quiet spot. The two friends shared Aunt Stanka's sausage and the remaining bread. They were out of water, but not of wine. They had a hearty drink and from then on they stopped being worried whatsoever. They decided not to stop until they reached X.

They passed another checkpoint, this time manned by the police. There, they were again warned to reconsider their journey further as two officers of the Secret Police had been captured in a nearby village. However, this did not impress the two friends much. The wine they had drunk instead of water made them more determined than ever. The political events in the country no longer concerned them. They had a goal – to reach X and have Jean cleared up of the mobilization.

Finally, they entered the town, and just in time, as Memo was starting to get drunk and if they had to drive another ten kilometers, they would probably have had to sleep in the Trabant. It was late afternoon, and it was getting dark. Jean had to guide his friend through the streets to the apartment. When they arrived, they parked the car in front of the house and, staggering, went inside.

There, Jean's landlady, Aunt Penny, welcomed them. She was wearing a velvet robe with big red roses and was just lighting the stove. When she saw the two young men enter the room, tottering, she made a disapproving grimace and said:

'Great job! What's going on here? You both smell like a walking distillery. When did you find time to get drunk?'

'Hello, Aunt Penny,' Jean began to stammer, 'this is Memo. He drove me here and he'll be sleeping in my room if you don't mind. But now we have to go to the military.'

'I bet you are going, right, boy? It's already six o'clock in the evening!' Her voice became shrill, as if she was deliberately overacting. 'There's not a living soul there at this hour. You can go tomorrow morning. And besides, it'll be better if you sober up!'

After that, Aunt Penny led them to the kitchen and served them dinner. She had cooked pork and cabbage stew. The two friends devoured two plates each, constantly praising the landlady's cooking skills. Aunt Penny seemed visibly charmed by the young men. They helped her clear the table and then sat in the living room to smoke a cigarette before bed.

Aunt Penny was already in a better mood. She was about her fifties or maybe a bit older. Jean never knew her exact age, and she carefully kept it a secret. Although she was aging, her facial features were well-preserved, and it was evident that she had once been a beautiful woman in her youth. Years ago, she had been imprisoned in the Belene labour camp for pimping, so she had extensive experience with the institutions of the communist state. As Jean mentioned to his friend, she was all but an ordinary citizen. She knew important people in the town's communist organization and other institutions as well, and would flawlessly resolve any problems she could encounter. Therefore, Jean was listening carefully to her advice on how to approach the military on the next day if he wanted to avoid the draft.

'Don't let yourself talk too much! Get yourself lower than grass. It's very important you do not stand out and not get philosophical, so you don't make them angry. There's a rule: to get out of the current, you have first to let it take you.' And that was Aunt Penny's advice, and when she finished, she quickly gulped down her glass of wine. 'Now, off to bed! You'll need all your strength for tomorrow. And for you, Memo, I have a separate room. Don't worry, you'll have a place to sleep over.'

Jean did not need much time to fall asleep. The whole day had been incredibly exhausting, and the alcohol had taken its toll. He had not even taken off his clothes when he started snoring.

The alarm clock went off at exactly five thirty in the morning. Jean woke up feeling rested and calm. It was dark outside. Through the window, he could see the bakery across the street, and he could make out the silhouettes of the bakers preparing breakfasts. Suddenly, he felt hungry and decided to run out and buy some banitsas[19] and boza[20] for the three of them. When he returned, he

---

[19] Banitsa – a traditional pastry made in Bulgaria. It is prepared by layering a mixture of whisked eggs, plain yogurt, and pieces of white brined cheese between filo pastry and then baking it in an oven.

[20] Boza – a fermented beverage originating from Central Asia and made throughout the Balkans, Turkey, Central Asia, the Caucasus, and North Africa. It is a malt drink made by fermenting various grains (in Bulgaria rye is usually used).

headed to the kitchen and heard the door to Aunt Penny's room creak. *Wow, she's up really early today*, Jean wondered. But his surprise was even greater when he saw Memo's tousled head poking through the door as he tiptoed out.

'What the hell were you doing?' Jean asked.

'Well, you know… Last night... after you fell asleep... we drank some more and... you know...' Memo explained guiltily.

Jean knew Aunt Penny well and was aware of her soft spot for younger men, but the whole situation seemed very comical to him. He was even more amused when he heard his landlady snoring from her room while Memo was closing the door. The two of them laughed and went to eat their banitsas.

But Jean's good mood gradually began to fade, replaced by a feeling of unease. He knew what was coming and felt those cold shivers down his spine again. Somehow, this whole situation had to come to an end.

The two friends got dressed and set off in the Trabant to the district military office. The dawn was breaking already. The wind was dying down, but the cold still had gripped everything around. The air was icy and piercing, as if it was cutting into their chests and reaching deep into their bodies.

They arrived at the military office location and parked. Memo wished his friend good luck and stayed in the Trabant waiting. In front of the military district building, a young soldier was standing on guard. Jean introduced himself and the soldier directed him further. When he entered the building, he saw at least thirty people in line and realized he had not come too early, but rather too late. These people were anxiously waiting to enter the room at the end of the corridor to talk to some kind of boss. *What a drag,* Jean thought, *everyone here wants to be discharged. And everyone has come up with some kind of excuse. Cunning foxes!,* he thought angrily. It seemed to him that he waited for an eternity, but finally, his turn came.

As soon as Jean had stepped over the threshold, it seemed all of Aunt Penny's advice abandoned him and he panicked and started tripping over chairs on the way. Cold sweat broke out on his forehead, but eventually he somehow managed to regain his composure. Along with him, a man of about forty entered. He was wearing a fur coat, and underneath he wore a pair of Western-brand jeans and a denim shirt. All of this impressed Jean, as in those days such clothes could hardly be obtained on the market.

Across them, behind an old, battered desk, sat an elderly colonel with graying mustaches and small round glasses. The two future reservists stood respectfully in front of him, and the colonel looked at them distrustfully and ordered them to introduce themselves, pointing to Jean first. Jean had rehearsed in his head a hundred times everything he needed to say, but at that moment he began to spout out scattered sentences in a voice hoarse from tension:

'Comrade Colonel,' Jean uttered, as though struggling for his breath, 'I'm going to be an engineer... uh... I won't be useful to you anyway... uh... I'm a student...'

'Shut up!' the colonel interrupted sharply. 'Who asked if you'll be useful or not?! I ordered you to introduce yourself. All of you are trying to get out of here. What kind of student are you?'

'Well... I'm a construction... you know, an engineer... and...'

'So you're a student, but not an engineer yet?' the colonel interrupted angrily.

'Well, no... just a bit more and I'll be one... you see... one exam left and...'

'Silence!' the colonel snapped. 'When you become an engineer, then you can philosophize. And you, who are you, what's your trade?' he pointed at the man in the fur coat.

'I'm a croupier, Comrade Colonel,' the man answered.

'Repeat!' the colonel demanded, but now his tone was rather confused than harsh.

'I'm a croupier,' the man in the fur coat repeated nervously. It was clear he also wanted to avoid the draft, but he was still rather composed, unlike Jean. 'I work at the Star Dream Hotel, in the Dew Complex."

Obviously, it was the first time ever the colonel had heard the word "croupier". There was silence. The military man thought for another moment and then turned to Jean:

'You see? That's how I want you to answer me. This man is a croupier, and you haven't even finished university. How dare you pretend to be an engineer. You're going to the draft!'

Jean's knees buckled. The worst-case scenario had come true. He did not have the strength to argue anymore. The colonel was visibly pleased that he had put "that arrogant engineer who was not even an engineer yet" in his place. The two men continued to stand in front of the desk.

The colonel relaxed a bit, however the word *croupier* could not leave his head. He wanted to understand a little more about this "title", but he also did not want to make a fool of himself. So he turned back to the man in the fur coat.

'Tell me how your work as a *croupier* is going!' he began, trying to avoid asking the question directly so as not to tip off "the two rascals".

The croupier's reaction, however, was unexpected for both the colonel and Jean.

'Well, how can I tell you?!' he exclaimed. 'I'm not sure how to answer your question!'

At that moment, it became clear that he had only been pretending to be calm.

A thin smile appeared on Jean's face, as if he had already accepted his fate. The colonel stood up, pounded his fist on the old desk, and ordered the croupier to be quiet. He was furious. His chin trembled with rage, and he chewed on the end of his mustache. He stormed out of the room and slammed the door. He wanted to hide his anger, which was caused by his own ignorance and by that "arrogant croupier". Jean and the other man still stood at attention, waiting. They did not speak, but the croupier could see the mocking expression on the face of the future engineer. After a few minutes, the colonel reentered, red with rage:

'You, the croupier, you're going to the draft along with the engineer. Now get out of here, both of you!'

The croupier seemed to crumble. He still had not realized what had just happened, but Jean nudged him lightly with his elbow and quietly urged him to go:

'Congratulations, smarty-pants! Now, off you go!'

And so ended the whole ordeal of mobilization. Jean spent about a month and a half in the reserves, in an old barracks, but absolutely nothing happened. All his fears turned out to be unfounded. He had taken his textbook with him and managed to prepare for the upcoming exam. He also made new friends, so the time passed quickly.

Things were unraveling not that good for the croupier, however. As soon as he arrived at the barracks, everyone had already heard about him and had nicknamed him "The Croupier", which he apparently did not like, and he was constantly arguing with people about it.

After the mobilization, Jean graduated and fulfilled his dream of working as a civil engineer. He was good at his specialty and was successful. He moved to live in the capital, where he witnessed the victory of democracy.

But both Jean and Memo were unprepared for the change. They had grown up under communism and expected to follow in the footsteps of their parents. Now something was happening that they had never even considered. Neither of them had any idea what would happen next. One thing was clear - that all of this meant a new start in the lives of both of them, and they believed that it was for the better.

AN ILLNESS AND THEREAFTER

Varna is a beautiful city – it was beautiful in the past and still is, in the present. Visiting Bulgaria but skipping Varna is unthinkable! The sea and the harbour have always imparted some distinctive ambiance to the city and a character to the people living there.

During the communist period, Varna was perhaps the most charming, clean and thriving city in the then "prosperous" country – a true model of the high standard and quality of life that the Communist Party had achieved for the population's welfare. Nevertheless, Varna was just the showcase to impress the "decaying" capitalism personified there by the Western tourists who used to visit the country during summer, attracted by the wonderful nature, the sea and the low prices. Back then, Varna stood out distinctively from the small country towns and villages, and that difference was obvious even to the ordinary citizens. It was not uncommon for countryside people coming for a holiday, to what was then called *the sea capital of the country*, to come upon some goods in the shops that they had never seen before.

In the summers, if the surging tourists were counted, the city along with its adjacent resorts could reach a million inhabitants. This used to bring some lovely bustle and fantastic mood. People would forget about all restrictions imposed on them, including the ban on visiting Western countries. They would disregard the relentless presence and control of the secret police, stalking everywhere, and finally start to feel free. During communism, the resorts of *Golden Sands* and *Friendship* were turned into luxurious places for Western tourists bringing in the then precious foreign currency.

Furthermore, Varna was an academic centre – the city was home to several universities that still exist today. At the beginning of the 1980s, the educational system was applying what was called *distribution of prospective students by region* – a "wise" decision, made by the higher party leadership, to have the university admission exams only held in the respective district where the prospective students come from. That meant that if you lived in the eastern part of the country, you could not study in the capital (in the western part), but only in a district town nearby – Varna, for example.

And it was for that reason that Anton Vasilev, a young man from a small provincial town, not far away from the Black Sea, became a student in medicine in Varna. He was excited and buoyant, and positive about his new life.

Tony, as his mates called him, wasn't one for grand pronouncements about the future. Brought up in a decent, tight-knit family who scraped by on a monthly wage, he had strong morals instilled in him. He had not travelled abroad, but found joy in listening to *Slade* and *Uriah Heep*. A real bookworm, he could devour a two-hundred-page novel in a day. A bit of a softie, he was a sensitive soul, perhaps a touch gullible at times.

Anton rarely failed to attend student shindigs. They had unforgettable evenings, dancing and drinking. And since the two best resorts on the Black Sea coast at that time, *Golden Sands* and *Friendship,* were a mere ten to twenty kilometre hop away from the city, such parties were often transferred there. All this fascinated Tony's gentle and sensitive soul while he began reckoning Varna as the ideal city to live in. He had realised where the difference between the folk in that town by the sea, and the rest of the country did come from – here they looked like being part of the free world.

In summertime, *Golden Sands* and *Friendship* were transformed and Anton liked spending more time there, in what his eyes saw as a whole new world. He'd watch, ever curious, as the foreign tourists strolled about, carefree and kitted out in brightly coloured outfits made of proper fabrics. They were having a good time, celebrating, enjoying the lovely sea and their lives. For their comfort, the communist government had established certain perks, such as special shops, called *Corecom*, stocked with foreign goods, where the locals were not allowed to shop. Travel companies, on the other hand, kept them entertained with picnics and trips to the casinos.

The hotels they stayed in were usually off limits to Bulgarians, but somehow there were local men and women who managed to start an affair with a foreigner or even get married. This practically meant a passport to the free world. Easy or not, it happened sometime, and left the families and friends of the lucky ones blatantly envious.

There were numerous entertainments for the tourists, one of which had particularly impressed Tony. Near one of the resorts, a small plane used to fly over the sea at lunchtime, and parachutists jumped out of it, landing skillfully on the beach just in front of the beachgoers.

Every summer, many students flocked to the *Golden Sands* and *Friendship* resorts to work. The jobs they took were typically part of the "Komsomol Labour Brigades", a popular government-led program during the communist era. Participation in these brigades was practically mandatory for university students and students and pupils from high schools and junior high schools. The pay was minimal, rather symbolic. Universities and schools formed the brigades during summers and autumns. Most of the work involved agriculture or service jobs in resorts. These brigades had a distinct structure with leaders and commanders at local, district, and national level. Despite being called "voluntary", participation therein was not truly optional. Unexcused absences could lead to serious consequences, potentially jeopardising a student's or pupil's ability to continue their education.

Despite all the work, those youthful hives would also offer plenty of fun. Evenings, after job done, saw dancing and music fill the air, fostering budding romances among the young people.

In his fourth year in the university, Anton had landed a leadership role as the commander of one such Komsomol brigade. This particular brigade was mostly made up of med students who spent their summer working various service jobs – waiting tables at restaurants, housekeeping at hotels, or assisting at the laundries. It turned out to be the most wonderful summer of Anton's life. His uniform, a simple blue shirt and trousers, came with a badge of authority: a red three-star insignia, signifying his status as a commander. His deputies wore similar ones, but with two stars only. One of them was briefly nicknamed DCPA, which stood for "Deputy Commander for Political Affairs."

Tony had a lot of fun, himself often being the unintended audience for some pretty hilarious scenes at his colleagues' work stations. One day, he had bumped into a familiar face – his neighbour, an old retiree – who was policing the area surrounding the hotels, collecting a motley crew of lost items: towels, bathing suits, jeans – all those being casualties fallen off the balconies, mostly after storms or strong winds, when the bounty was even more plentiful. The old man confessed this had been his regular routine for years.

Although the seaside town was beautiful and spotless, Anton never managed to accustom to the coastal climate. Damp winter months caused him bronchitis, sinusitis, pneumonia, all that stuff. During his third winter there, he got struck down with a nasty bout of pneumonia, landing him in hospital.

The pulmonary clinic was housed in an old building, which resembled a barn that had been converted into a hospital. The hospital room was small, barely squeezing in the four beds.

Suddenly, once a medical student, now Tony had changed into a frightened patient. That role was not familiar to him yet, so he began seeing the flip side of life. At night, as he was falling asleep, he could hear the footsteps of nurses and orderlies in the corridor. One evening, he even saw a dead man being carried out of the next room, and everything inside him turned upside down. Life acquired such dimensions he had never been aware of before; he realised that no one was untouchable.

The doctors and nurses in the ward were attentive and filled with compassion for the patients. The hospital room Tony was assigned to already had three other patients. One was an elderly man who had accidentally ingested paint thinner and was now recovering from a severe esophageal burn; the man was roaming incessantly the corridor, muttering something incomprehensible. The other one was rather quiet, but Tony heard that he, just like him, had pneumonia. The third man, Ivan, was about 45 years old, had a pale face and streaked black hair that had started to bald near his temples. He had a powerful frame and looked like an energetic man. Restless in the room, he frequently went out to the terrace for a smoke. Anton couldn't help but notice Ivan was smoking *Kent* – cigarettes, which at that time could usually be bought at *Corecom* only. Already two weeks into the hospital for coughing, Ivan's X-rays were not showing any improvement, according to the doctors.

The first few days in the hospital Anton had high fever and he sweated constantly. He felt weak and even getting out of bed left him slightly breathless. Fear crept in – his family was away, and he started feeling utterly alone and vulnerable. Just then, Ivan stepped in – with uncanny intuition, he sensed Anton's emotional turmoil and offered him encouragement and support, helping him fight his illness, even predicting his pending recovery.

Twice a day, Ivan's wife would come to the hospital, together with their children, to bring him home-cooked meals, fresh fruit juices and mineral water. They always invited Tony to join them for lunch and soon he felt like a member of that warm and close-knit family.

A long week marred by fear in the ward passed and gave way to Anton's recovery. His fever subsided, and his cough faded.

Without much thought, he found himself smoking on the terrace with his newfound friend, engaging in hours-long, unburdened conversations about life, Ivan's illness, and about the upcoming additional examination he was scheduled for – a bronchoscopy that would shed some light on his condition.

On the day Tony was about to be discharged from the hospital, his friend's test results revealed a devastating diagnosis – he had lung cancer, and a thoracic surgeon was called from the ward for consultation. Surgery was deemed necessary.

Ivan was a man of unwavering fortitude, not succumbing to despair or shedding tears, and the very mention of the surgery filled him with aversion. Anton, a mere third-year medical student, was consumed by a fervent desire to aid his friend, whom he had known for just a fortnight. He was trying to convince Ivan that all would be well after the operation.

Ivan's wife had unconditionally acknowledged Tony as an expert and relied completely on his advice. The surgery was over, but the outcome was far from what the family and Tony had anticipated. The tumour had enlarged, and the doctors were unable to remove it entirely. Ivan had declined both radiation and chemotherapy and began to live his life as before. He had ample financial means and appeared free from material worries.

Anton had realised that his friend belonged to a suspicious group of people, who during the communist time were called *changers*. They were involved in illegal purchases of US dollars and other western currencies from foreigners, reselling it afterwards.

In Varna, these people had their own area of operations, or "work stations", in the downtown area. They did not have jobs, nor did they study but rather earned a living from their currency exchange business, always selling well-above the official rate announced by the national bank.

Of course, all these dollars, francs, and pounds often ended up at the *Corecom* stores, where they were spent for apparel, perfumes, alcohol, cigarettes, and other similar stuff. The employees at these stores usually turned a blind eye, prioritising sales over proof of origin for the currency, otherwise required by the Bulgarian citizens. Following that pattern, Anton had managed to acquire a denim jacket, a shirt, and jeans – a deed he considered a great success. As someone had joked back then, *Corecom* stood for "correction of communism." Later, this very wit was reportedly fired from his job.

In the aftermath of the surgery, Ivan had grappled with the reality of his situation, yet he resolved to carry on as before. One day, he called Tony, and they arranged a meeting in downtown Varna, in front of the *Black Sea Hotel*. Upon their reunion, they embraced like brothers and sat on a bench, the vast expanse of the sea stretching out before them. Ships were at anchor in the bay, boats as well, and from their vantage point they could see the entire beach unfolding before them. People from all corners of the globe were strolling along the promenade.

'Hi, mate!' Ivan started, his voice faint and with a wheeze.

'Hi!' answered Tony, his heart sinking with grief.

'Don't pity me, please, I'm just a sick man, that's all,' Ivan sensed his feelings and then continued: 'Doctor, please, can you find me an oxygen tank? I feel like I'm suffocating when I'm going to bed at night.

Tony nodded silently, his throat constricting as if deprived of air. He really liked Ivan and was struggling to grasp the harsh reality.

'I just don't wanna go to the hospital, that's all. I don't want all those needles and IVs. I just want to be with my family, till the end. I need to go now, but before I do, there's something I want to share with you. I don't know why, but I feel the need to tell you this…'

And he began:

'In the mid-70s, I decided to escape from Bulgaria and go to Western Europe. I tried with an organised trip first, but they wouldn't let me go. I made an attempt by getting on a ship, but they caught me and then put me in jail. I became a sort of a political prisoner. There were many like me among the political prisoners. However, with a friend of mine, we managed to escape from prison, swam across the Danube River, and headed for Austria. The heat was scorching and we were starving. We avoided villages and roads, and we ate whatever we could find. I should tell you about my companion – that was his second attempt to escape to the West as well. Anyway, at one point we could already see the Austrian border and we lay down in a cornfield. But just our luck – pigs appeared out of nowhere, grunting, and gave us away. What a farce, mate, I could see Austria, my heart was pounding so hard I thought it would burst, but I was caught again and sent back to Bulgaria. Then, of course, they threw me back in prison and after a while they let me go. I never saw the free world, mate… Goodbye now and I wish you all the best,' Ivan finished.

Then he stood up, inhaled deeply and slowly walked away on the street. They never met again.

Some time later, Tony met Ivan's wife and learned that Ivan had passed away.

Back then, no one believed that democracy would ever prevail, no one could even imagine such a future.

Eventually, Anton witnessed the fall of communism and became a free man, yet memories continued to haunt him. Upon retirement, he often walked to the *Black Sea Hotel*, spending hours on the same bench, gazing at the sea. Ivan had departed this world, but left in Anton's soul memories of dignity and courage. In hindsight, Anton realised that his friend had triumphed over evil. *Only craving for a free life can justify history,* he thought sometimes, when recalling the late Ivan.

Now, Varna is a city of free people, who hardly remember that past. And that's all right.

TWO CAPTAINS AND A CIVILIAN

For the larger part of men in Bulgaria, meeting up with friends for a glass of grape rakia and a Shopska[21] salad is a social norm. Depending on the mood, a couple of glasses of "grapy" might be consumed, and they would usually go with one or two salads, whereas the number of salads does not necessarily correspond to the number of glasses of rakia. The Shopska salad is our unique, Bulgarian *magnum opus*. It features fresh cucumbers, tomatoes, and onions, which are carefully chopped and then thoroughly covered with grated white brined cheese. Nothing beats the taste of this salad, especially if the vegetables have been picked early in the same morning.

You can hardly find a Bulgarian who does not adore the Shopska salad. It is an icon of our cuisine and has become a representative of our national menu, highly favoured among the majority of tourists visiting the Bulgarian Black Sea coast. At any restaurant, tradition calls for ordering a Shopska salad whenever you

---

[21] A traditional Bulgarian salad made of tomatoes, cucumbers, green peppers (sometimes charred or baked), onions, parsley and white brined cheese.

order a glass of rakia with. In the past, if a customer would forget it, the waiter would always remind him with a rhetorical question, "What about a Shopska salad, perhaps?"

Although it might be challenging to coax a Western tourist to try grape rakia, we must say, the same does not go for the Shopska salad – they simply adore it. There are many other types of salads, but Shopska has earned its reputation as the menu's perfect complement to a glass of good old rakia.

In the past, restaurants used to offer several types of rakia: grape, apricot, and pear. However, grape rakia was the universally admired liquor queen. The masters who distilled rakia focused on its taste and aroma. Regardless of whether it was produced in home stills or state-owned distilleries, it would always bring Bulgarian men together at the table.

Traditionally, a rakia drink was reserved for the evenings, after work, at home, but very often also in a restaurant, on the way home. Dinner meals would often be postponed after men got home, much to the annoyance of their wives who would again have to deal with their "lawful beloved's" tipsy state. The "rakia-connoisseurs" would never go straight for a main meal before they turned over a couple of glasses of rakia accompanied by a Shopska salad, which – when at home, and depending on the season – could be substituted for pickles.

And so, one evening at the Rodopi[22] restaurant tradition had gathered three friends for a glass of "grapy" and a Shopska salad. The Rodopi restaurant was located in the center of our small provincial town and served as a kind of an intersection for all the three men's routes on their way home. They often gathered, with or without a reason, to drink and chat. They usually sat in a corner of the restaurant, which had about twenty tables, carefully arranged and covered with red striped tablecloths, greasy stains here and there.

The establishment had two sections – an indoor area and a garden. The indoor part of the restaurant had high windows that were left wide open in the summer, while in the winter, heavy red draperies, cigarette smoke lingering within, were lowered behind them. Here, with Bulgarian pop tunes playing, people would leave their worries behind and chat about anything, forgetting all their troubles and work stress. Everyone had their own dreams, which would differ from the dreams of others. It was the end of the 1970s, and the courage of Bulgarians was somehow beginning to rise.

The three friends were regulars at the Rodopi restaurant. Captain Tsonko Chereshov was a full-time Secret Police officer, and that fact was no secret to either of his two companions, or to the restaurant's staff. While nobody knew the specifics of his job – and he had never discussed it – the mere fact that he was an officer in the

---

[22] The Rhodopes (Bulgarian: Rodopi) are a mountain range in Southeastern Europe, and the largest by area in Bulgaria.

secret police was enough to inspire fear in people at that time. Yet, despite the difference in their positions, following an unspoken rule the friendship of our three characters would always come first.

Being friends with Chereshov was not an easy business. After graduating from the police school, later renamed an academy, his ego grew too high. His salary was higher than the salaries of his friends, and soon he even bought a new car – a Lada. It was a Soviet-made super-limousine, emblematic of Eastern European countries at the time.

Later, Chereshov took advantage of the opportunity that had been provided to police officers and graduated from a part-time university course in law studies. Then, after passing equivalency exams at that same police academy, he managed to obtain a law degree. Later, this would incidentally turn out to be a lifeline for him and most officers like him, who were retired after the democratic changes in the country. Eventually, they would not end up on the streets, but would become lawyers instead, or legal advisers to banks or insurance companies, etc. After the fall of communism, Chereshov would also found his own law firm.

Unlike other policemen, Tsonko enjoyed more privileges at the time. He was allowed to dress in civilian clothes instead of the otherwise obligatory uniform, and also to skip the sports events in the police. Moreover, for him, it was not mandatory to shave every day, so he also had a beard, which he rather kept because of being slovenly than being dandyish. In short, he possessed an independence that distinguished him from the rest of the police officers.

He used to spend his entire days in cafés. Before noon, he would drink three or four coffees, trying to read the new newspapers from cover to cover. After five in the evenings, when the workday officially ended for everyone, Tsonko would move to the Rodopi restaurant and here he would find citizens from different social strata who would treat him to a drink. That way, Chereshov was building relationships and positions in society, and perhaps worked on his secret stuff or something, but who knows.

He was a quiet, private guy, and his job only made him even more reserved, so he would never say more than he needed to. But among friends and especially after a third drink in a row, he would become loquacious, even loud at times. His wife did not have a clue where he was going, when he would return, or how drunk he would be. Over the years, the poor woman had learned to live with her circumstances. As Tsonko would say as an excuse or as an explanation, 'Work is done over drinks, and if I want to keep going up in my job, I have to keep up with the drinking rhythm of the bosses.'

It must be admitted that Captain Chereshov would gladly drink up a bottle of rakia without moving from his place. Usually, afterwards, he would get up from the table, shake out his greenish overcoat, and set off, unruffled, home or to some unknown destination elsewhere.

His two friends, who often shared a table with him, knew his habits well. One was Kaun Stanimirov, an agronomist. He worked at the newly created agro-industrial complex, better known as AIC[23], and had been a classmate of Chereshov from the time they were in first grade at school.

Kaun was forty, short and overweight. He had never done any physical labor in his life and had never made an effort to exercise. When he had to walk quickly, he would get out of breath from carrying around all that weight. He had had a brief stint as a field agronomist, perhaps the only time in his life he had done any real physical work. He had quickly climbed the career ladder, first becoming vice-chairman, and later chairman of the local agro-industrial complex. This secured a comfortable life for him for years to come. He stayed in his second-floor office, went on inspections to nearby villages in the government car, and then returned home with

---

[23] *Agro-Industrial Complex* – this is an "invention" of the Bulgarian Communist Party dating back to the end of the 1960s and the beginning of 1970s, which generally comprises a larger farming unit and a smaller industrial one. The aim was to procure a larger ratio of the working class (typical for a civic environment) in the typically agrarian rustic areas, while still preserving (and increasing) the level of farm production in the respective regions.

crates full of fresh produce, pilfered from the state's land for his family and friends. His wife was also an agronomist, but she actually worked in the fields.

During the summer, when the fruit in the complex's garden ripened, Kaun would bring a couple of crates of hand-picked peaches and cherries to his friend Tsonko, so he could make compotes and jam. In the fall, he would supply him with top-quality grapes for wine. Captain Chereshov liked to make two to three hundred liters of wine and at least fifty liters of brandy. Well-stocked with homemade alcohol, Tsonko was confident about getting through the coming winter. No one ever figured out if he paid for the grapes and, if so, at what price.

The third member of the company was Orlin Keleshev, an army captain, a friend of theirs, with whom they had once been classmates as well, albeit from different classes. Kelesh, as he was called, had graduated from a military school with a specialization in "Ground Forces", meaning he was a foot soldier or a *Kashik*[24] as they were popularly known. After graduation, however, his father went to plead with important comrades in the military district and in the district party committee, and eventually managed to arrange for his son to be reassigned to a secret military unit. This did not match his qualifications at all, but it apparently did not bother anyone.

---

[24] Similar to English *tommy*.

Keleshev was an actual athlete. Every morning, he would go for a five-kilometer jogging, and afterwards, back at the barracks, he would play football with his fellow officers. He never missed a workout on the pull-ups and dips bars station, where he would do pull-ups, while his favourites were the parallel bars where he was doing dips – he could do up to a hundred dips without stopping. All this was a kind of a personal measure of endurance and training for the military, and naturally it boosted Keleshev's confidence. Like Chereshov, he was also a discreet person and did not really like to talk about his work in front of others.

The three buddies used to comply with an unspoken agreement: they would not ask each other about work or how their day had passed. Their go-to topics were women and, if they had had enough rakia – then politics. But once the alcohol kicked in, all professional boundaries and unspoken rules would go out through the window.

That particular frosty Friday night was no different. It was past ten, pitch black outside, and the town was dead. Every now and then, a shadow would slip past under the streetlights, and the air was thick with that particular, stale coal-burning smell, as people then used mainly coal for heating.

At that bleak background, the Rodopi restaurant was a whole different story. The place was teeming with people, the music was pumping, and everyone was having a blast. Waiters were running around the tables, balancing trays piled high with drinks and dishes full of meatballs and kebabs. The air was thick with cigarette smoke.

The three friends had taken their usual spot in the corner and were raising toasts with grape rakia, glass after glass. They had already ditched the unspoken rules and were talking freely. Tsonko Chereshov's laughter would boom occasionally, accompanied by the clinking sound of glasses usually following just another toast. Before they knew it, several hours had flown by. Then the music started to fade, a subtle hint from the restaurant's maître d'hôtel that it was time for the guests to wrap things up.

Kaun looked at his watch and mumbled, 'Huh? But it's already ten to twelve. Anyway... that's alright; at least my wife will be asleep by now. I'm tired of giving her explanations.' And he raised his glass to finish his rakia.

Keleshev just yawned and waved his hand.

But Chereshov, who was just lighting up a cigarette, turned abruptly to the agronomist and looked at him intently with his alcohol-reddened eyes. The other man looked back at him without blinking, and so a few seconds passed in which the two stared at each other with drunken gazes. Then Kaun noticed that Chereshov's eyes seemed to be welling up, but he also began to feel like he was going to cry himself, even though he did not have any idea why. Chereshov slowly exhaled a thick cloud of smoke and, leaning towards the agronomist, asked out of the blue:

'Do you know, my friend, that my uncle was killed while he was a member of the resistance?' And he stared inquisitively into Kaun's red eyes, which were as though they were actually starting to get teary.

The reply came immediately: 'I don't know that,' Kaun mumbled.

The rakia had gotten to him and he was having trouble speaking.

'But what's the big deal? The man is dead... it's really a shame that he didn't live to see the victory.'

'Yes... he'd gone... too soon...' Chereshov was feeling sentimental, and it was obvious that this topic was likely to be discussed for quite a while. After exhaling another cloud of smoke, he continued, 'But this gave me the opportunity to apply to the police academy and get accepted without any obstacles! Did you know that, Orlin?' he turned to his other companion.

Keleshev, who was about to nod off, suddenly shot up like he had been zapped. He paused for a moment, as if considering something. It was obvious that he did not know this fact, but something clicked in his consciousness, and his face contorted with malice: 'I knew something was up with you getting into the secret police. I applied twice and was rejected. I knew it... I got rejected because of people like you!'

'Listen, Kelesh,' Chereshov shouted, 'my uncle was a resistance squad commander and was killed in 1943. You must know that!' continued the Secret Police officer. 'And know that it wasn't him who helped me, but *I myself* applied and *I was accepted* into the service,' Chereshov roared even louder, slightly rising from his chair with his hand on the pistol hanging at his waist. 'While your grandfather, Kelesh, was a resistance aid, right? Why – I'm asking you – were you not accepted, tell me Keleshev? Do you know why? Two reasons! First – you lack what it takes to be an officer of the services, and second, more importantly – your grandfather was a coward. He became an aid to the resistance, but it was already on the 8th of September, just a day before the 9th[25], you know... That was him: a wimp!'

The conversation had taken a bad turn, and the guests at the neighboring tables began paying their bills and quickly leaving the restaurant. Everyone knew that these two would not just mess around: now, Keleshev was also gripping his holster. The waiter at their table became even more attentive, making sure not to miss a word of the conversation. Meanwhile, the maître d'hôtel skillfully

---

[25] The 1944 Bulgarian coup d'état took place on the 9th of September.

wrapped a bottle of red wine in an old newspaper and slipped out through the back door, unnoticed.

Kaun was sitting between the two of them, baffled by his friends' behaviour – this was something that had never occurred, so far, between them. It was clear that tonight, everyone had overdone it with the drinking; or – perhaps – the two captains had started celebrating the coming weekend even earlier – as far back as lunchtime. Kaun strained his foggy mind and realized that the only people left in the restaurant were himself, the two captains, and the terrified waiter. And that was when he felt he needed to say something to calm them down, and suddenly, he remembered a story that his grandfather – already long deceased – had told him years ago.

'Listen, pals,' Kaun stammered with a crooked smile. But Chereshov had already picked up steam and rudely cut him off:

'Say it, you empty-headed squash!' he laughed. 'You, pumpkin head! And that's exactly what your name is, right[26]?'

Kaun either didn't hear the insult, or pretended not to, and persevered unwaveringly with the story:

---

[26] Kaun – in some parts of Bulgaria that is a dialect word for any sort of melon, water-melon, pumpkin or squash.

'During the Second World War, my grandfather, the old Kaun, was drafted. Poor old man,' the agronomist teared up and wiped his greasy face with his sleeve, 'he had three daughters and two sons. He himself had never cared much for politics or the war... you know... he was just a gardener. He had his own garden, growing fruits and vegetables to make a living. The man worked hard to educate his children because he had become well-off... but in a fair way, by means of proper labour,' the agronomist kept stammering impetuously, wiping his snotty nose with a napkin. 'And just when he was thinking things were finally looking up, guess what? He was mobilized. His whole life, everything he'd built – was gone... just like that... He had to leave behind his family, his home, his wife – everything. And he was having enough money to live comfortably instead. In the end, hard luck dragged him to the frontlines, and he – a simple gardener – saw a rifle for the first time, so to say. And then the worst part came!'

Here, the agronomist could not stop wiping away his drunken tears and continued in a trembling voice.

'The first battle at the front! Everyone was lined up in the trenches, waiting for the signal. Meanwhile, Grandpa was looking through his binoculars, seeing nothing. He looked, but all he could think about was home, his children, and his garden. Then, something clicked up in his head, and he decided that somehow he had to get out of this nightmare. While he was thinking this, he suddenly heard the signal. His battalion was ordered to attack the enemy's fortified positions. Everyone jumped up with a battle cry. Only Grandpa remained in the trench, cowering. Every one of his comrades who stood up was shot and fell. Grandpa trembled all over but did not lose his composure and quickly decided he wasn't going to die. So he hid in the trench, among the dead, and lay still. He could hear the bullets whizzing by and the shells exploding, but he figured the chance of being killed by a shell in the trench was less than if he got up with the others to attack. Then, out of nowhere, the company commander appeared and started yelling at him: "Attack! Kaun, get up, you dirty dog!" But Grandpa didn't move. He lay in the trench, his face buried in the ground. When the company commander saw he wasn't budging, he pulled out his pistol and started threatening him with a court-martial, but even that didn't work. Then the sergeant came to help, and the two of them started kicking Grandpa, but poor guy, he just clung tighter to the ground. He decided he would rather take a beating than die. He even calculated that if they put him in prison, he'd be out in some ten years... alive! Finally, they left him lying in the trench and went on with the rest. After four or five hours, the attack ended, and there was silence. Only then did Grandpa rise from the trench. He looked around and moved forward to the new position his company had captured. He was so scared, poor guy, that he didn't even notice everyone was laughing at him. Eventually, he avoided the court-martial. After that battle, their company was pulled back to the rear, and so Grandpa survived. Years ago, they had invited him to school to tell the pupils his war stories, but he didn't go. "Fortunately," he once told me, "there's no one from my company in town." You see, no one was there to expose him. He even passed as a war veteran. But that's how the old man died – concerned that someone would come up and disclose that disgraceful moment to his loved ones. So, pals, don't fight over nonsense,' Kaun concluded philosophically.

There was silence. No one had ever heard that story before. Usually, war stories were heroic and glorious, or at least tragic. The waiter, who was eavesdropping, froze in surprise, and the two captains were speechless. There was simply nothing more to say. It was midnight, so they quickly finished their drinks and left.

To be brave or to be cowardly? Kaun was pondering afterwards. He just wanted to forget this story – without judging his grandfather, without drawing any conclusions. He was glad to have helped his friends reconcile. They were part of his life, and he did not want that envy between them.

Time was passing, and the two captains and the civilian agronomist continued to meet at the Rodopi restaurant, drinking grape rakia with Shopska salad. The topic of Kaun's grandfather was never brought up again. All three of them had put themselves in his shoes, in the shoes of a man with five children and some money, who had forgotten his dignity and honor, just in order to survive. They had faced tough times in their lives, but they had not been to war, and none of them knew how they would have handled it. At least they stopped doing one thing! They stopped boasting about the achievements of their relatives.

After the fall of communism, they were retired and forgotten, but fate had been kind to all three of them – they never went to war.

PROFESSOR DRAGNI SHESTAKOV

Dragni Shestakov was born in the rural countryside, but as it would appear eventually, fortune favored him, and he went on to have a remarkable career as a doctor in the capital. His home village, Kickastone, no longer exists on the map.

In his youth, he was a skinny, zippy boy. Their family house was not large, although it was well-maintained, clean, and like most homes at the time, it had plastered walls and an outdoor toilet.

However, the family had a large yard attached to their small house, almost a quarter of an acre in size. Dragni's mother was a hardworking woman who had succeeded in turning their yard into a sort of a kitchen garden paradise, where together with her son, they carefully planted and tended to various vegetables. They tilled the soil, watered the plants, and put in a lot of effort, as the family used to sell much of their produce and make a living through that petty trade. They did not earn much, but as those familiar with our national character like to say: whatever they earned was just enough to keep food on the table and stave off hunger.

Back in the communist days, having anything for sale was a valuable routine. Every week, on a weekday, the town next to the village of Kickastone traditionally hosted a farmers' market where people from nearby villages would bring their produce – whatever they had grown – to sell. So, in his youth, Dragni had honed his skills in vegetable trading and it was obvious that he had a knack for selling cucumbers, tomatoes and cabbages. Probably those early experiences at the market laid the foundation for his future success – but who can say for sure...?

Dragni's mother was a typical village woman, incredibly hardworking and energetic, and literate: she could read and write. In addition to working in her garden, Aunt Yana also worked as a cook in the agricultural cooperative, so she could get food without needing to buy coupons for the village canteen. This, by the way, was very important to her, as it gave her stability and security in raising her son. She had no other children and Dragni flourished under her guidance. His father had passed away early and left him an orphan at a young age.

Notwithstanding his humble origin and unlike his peers, Dragni stood out for his exceptional love of learning. He graduated from the eighth grade with honors, and then repeated this success in the high school of the district town. These accomplishments fueled his ambition to study medicine in the capital later.

In university, dedication to his studies set him apart from his peers, often arousing envy in many, especially among the "native" Sofians, who never missed an opportunity to highlight his rural background and character. To some extent, there was some truth to their claims, as despite his undeniable love of learning and success, Dragni's soul remained deeply imbued with typical rustic cunning. By nature, he was a cheerful fellow, at times even bohemian. He loved large gatherings and drinking with friends and colleagues.

While at university, Dragni met his love - a fellow medical student, and eventually married her. She was an unassuming woman, but in his eyes, she possessed the most beautiful and noble quality – she was a native of Sofia, therefore she was entitled to Sofia right of residence[27].

Right of residence, a seemingly obscure and perhaps insignificant aspect of life in democratic countries, was a bureaucratic cornerstone in the administration of the communist state. In short, it meant that if someone was a resident of a particular

---

[27] During WW2 the Bulgarian government restricted the right of citizens to move to live in Sofia due to the housing shortage caused by the war. Later, after the war, the new communist rulers continued this policy calling it *Sofia right of residence*. According to that regulation, those who had that right of residence were only people who were already living in Sofia, while a person from another town or village would not be allowed to move to Sofia. The Sofia right of residence was given by the authorities at their discretion only, where preference was given mainly to people with special professions, skills and qualities, or to people who would marry someone who already had the right of residence. Thus, at the time, people from the country sought relations with people already living in Sofia. Many false marriages were organized for this reason as well.

town or village, they could only live and work in that town of village, and this was recorded in their passport[28]. Otherwise, it meant a bureaucratic nightmare, searching for the so-called "legal grounds" to start a job or simply live elsewhere – where one liked or where he considered it was best for his family.

After graduating from university, every young doctor was subject to a kind of distribution system for young specialists and had to go and work where a committee of administrators would assign them to. In most cases, this meant a village somewhere in the province. And Dragni, coming from a village himself, had no desire to return to another one. He enjoyed city life and was ambitious, but he lacked just that one small detail – the right of residence.

As a rule, medical school graduates who had excelled in their studies were granted the privilege of choosing the town, the hospital, and the specialty they wanted to pursue. Dragni was one of the top students in his class, but there were a couple of courses he had not quite aced – he claimed that a professor just did not like him because he thought Dragni was philosophizing too much, which

---

[28] In the communist times, every Bulgarian citizen over the age of fourteen had a passport. Despite possessing passports, their freedom of movement was restricted to domestic travel. These passports functioned primarily as identification documents, containing detailed personal information such as address, occupation, employer, parental names, and names of children, if any. These passports were issued by the police. The passport "giving the right for traveling abroad" was a totally different document, usually issued after a complicated procedure that included a check of the applicant's status performed by the secret police.

irritated him. In any case, Dr. Shestakov was denied the privilege of choosing the place where to work.

There was just another option left to stay in the capital: enrolling in an after-graduate program at the Medical Institute and completing a dissertation within a few years. Dragni carefully considered this option but quickly dismissed it after having witnessed a comical situation where a cousin of his, a graduate student, failed to complete his dissertation and was compelled to return to his hometown, humiliated.

Having weighed the options, he decided to stick with his original, more reliable plan and marry the aforementioned classmate. Nikolina, as his chosen one was called, was also eager to settle down after her graduation – to start a family, and have children. Respectively, it did not take Dragni long to realize this, and he quickly started to pursue her. And although his eyes would "wander" when other women were around, he persevered to the end and eventually carried out his plan.

Thus, the newly graduated doctor managed to "hack" the system and to triumph with a Sofia right of residence and a medical degree. This was a cornerstone in his biography, and his faithful wife found herself in the role of a springboard for the career of the future Professor Dragni Shestakov.

Once he obtained the right of residence, he began to live his own life. Although he had married with ulterior motives, he remained faithful to Nikolina and never considered leaving her or getting a divorce. They had a daughter whom he loved and cared for deeply, and that was just enough for his wife. Dragni remained true to the family values instilled in him as a child by his mother.

The stability in his family gave him security and support. With his personal life in order, he could now focus on his career. He specialized in one of the most prestigious clinics and established himself as a reliable doctor, trusted by his patients. When someone met him, they got the impression of a stable, serious, and professional man.

Over time, however, whether due to the complicated interpersonal relationships in the academic circles that he was moving within or the stressful and demanding nature of his work, Dragni's character underwent unexpected transformations. Dr. Shestakov – the future Professor Shestakov – developed his own survival tool for dealing with difficult and elaborate situations – he started to lie.

Initially, he used lies to impress women, but over the years, lying somehow became a part of his personality and even one of his traits. He became so entangled in lies that he started to lie even to his family. When he talked to someone, he could not resist telling a story from his life that had never actually happened.

For instance, one day in his later years, after he had already acquired the title of professor, he was on duty and told a young colleague a story about how, when he had acute appendicitis, a special helicopter was sent for him to take him to Marseille for the surgery. His listener was just nodding, doing the math in his head about the distance from Bulgaria to France and realizing the absurdity of Dragni's claim that a helicopter could have flown such a distance.

Another story was told by a nurse from the clinic who was spending her summer vacation at a famous Black Sea resort. One evening, in front of the restaurant, she unexpectedly met an old, long-time-not-seen acquaintance. After some small talk, he invited her to join their table to meet an extraordinary Bulgarian doctor who had served as a military medic during the war in former Yugoslavia. The woman was intrigued and gladly accepted the invitation, but she could not believe her eyes when she saw none other than Dragni Shestakov, dressed in a wide, orange Hawaiian shirt and short sky-blue pants with white side stripes, passionately recounting his wartime experiences and exploits, working in the battlefield conditions. Of course, she did not say a word about the fact that the professor had never set foot outside Bulgaria until then. The situation was comical. Dragni was intoxicated by his own tall tales, and his dinner companions were in awe of the bravery of that eminent Bulgarian doctor.

It was not uncommon for our distinguished character to astound his conversation companions by citing world facts and theories that no one had ever actually said.

One thing was sure however – everything that came out of his mouth sounded plausible and beyond doubt and only an "experienced" ear could detect his lies. But since those who knew him best were his colleagues and family, he never faced any opposition to the nonsense he used to forge throughout his lifetime.

This new addition to Dr. Shestakov's repertoire – lying – helped him build many useful connections and have important acquaintances. Having connections meant knowing people from the economic and political elite, the security services, or in responsible positions in government ministries, who could help you with anything in a difficult moment, including advancing your career.

Dragni was a good doctor, but there were a few things that were consistently holding him back in his development. One such drawback was that he did not speak any foreign language well. This might seem strange to the reader, but given the rapid pace of scientific development and the fact that the latest discoveries and innovations typically come from the wealthiest and most developed countries, the need to speak a foreign language is an unspoken rule. This was and still is the case in the academic circles of our small country. Unfortunately, during the communist era, the opportunity to study English was often reserved for the children of the political elite only.

Dragni coped with this as well as with some other obstacles by joining the Communist Party. Besides the right of residence in Sofia, Dragni greatly valued his wife because of her father as well. His father-in-law belonged to a special category of people who enjoyed the highest privileges and benefits in the state: the so-called "anti-fascist activist". In addition to being an anti-fascist activist, the man also worked in the district committee of the Communist Party.

Of course, Dr. Shestakov had calculated everything and was fully aware that without his father-in-law's connections, he would never advance or succeed. Therefore, Dragni maintained the warmest possible relations with him, and eventually he was rewarded. After playing his strongest card, Dragni's career skyrocketed. From an ordinary doctor in a hospital ward, he rose to become an assistant, one of the first steps within the academic community.

Dr. Shestakov gained confidence and, simply put, felt as if walking on air. Meanwhile, among his colleagues, a suspicion was growing that Dragni was somehow assisting the political secret services, which caused a certain degree of awe in them.

Even after the demise of communism and the onset of democratic changes in the country, this did not change. The new situation never bothered Dr. Shestakov too much, as "former" communists still held many important administrative positions, and he, so to speak, continued to swim in his own waters. And so, one morning he woke up as Associate Professor Shestakov, and a couple of years later, a sign with the inscription "Professor Shestakov" was already hanging on his office door.

There was another interesting element to the professor's aura. We, Bulgarians, know very well that important things in our country are always decided at the table. And, at the table, Professor Shestakov was just invincible. It could rightly be said that he mastered the art of eating and drinking to excess, and this quality played a significant role not only in his career but also in his social development. His dining companions were often amazed at his ability to consume large amounts of food without batting an eye.

One evening, during a big department party, Dragni had latched onto one of the new residents at the clinic and had "ensnared" him to fill his glass with alcohol and his plate with food whenever they got empty. The party had started around six in the evening and was in full swing, and every twenty or thirty minutes, the young doctor tirelessly added various dishes from the buffet to his mentor's plate while simultaneously refilling his glass with drinks. This continued until around midnight, when Professor Shestakov rose, unshaken, from his seat to the astonished gaze of the resident, saying:

'Come, my boy, walk me out.'

Without asking any questions, the young man helped him put on his overcoat. Then Dragni looked at his watch and, adjusting his hat, continued:

'Well, my boy, I'm leaving now. I don't wanna miss the last tram home. I'll see you tomorrow, at the office.'

And he quickly headed for the door, so as not to miss the last public transport. The young doctor watched him walk away and wondered what kind of a strange bird that professor was.

Over the years, Dragni's obsession for food continued to grow, eventually reaching gargantuan proportions. From a once slender and elegant young man, by the age of forty he had transformed into a solid, middle-aged man. His face had grown round, and his eyes seemed small. He had difficulty finding clothes that fit. At work, he spent most of his time wandering around the clinic in a medical coat that barely fastened around his waist. In the mornings, he would arrive early to have breakfast from the hospital food. Since these were the early years of the transition, patient meals were still prepared in the old way – the hospital had its own kitchen where food was cooked and then distributed to the wards.

As a rule, Dragni was not entitled to hospital food, but there would always be a patient being discharged from the hospital or a colleague on duty who was not hungry, so food could always be found for him. For dinner, the professor often arranged for a meal at the restaurant of friends; he rarely ate at home, because he liked to take "freebies".

Over time, Dragni managed to save some money and eventually bought his own place. Admittedly, it was not a big one, but it was his own. And here again, his "genius" showed through. The practical Professor Shestakov made his own architectural changes and partitions, turning the small apartment into a multi-room dwelling. But his ingenuity would not end there. When it came time to furnish his new home, he found friends who were privatizing several hotels in the capital and offered him to choose from the old furniture they were about to throw out.

And yet, Professor Shestakov had not been born a professor. For many years, he had been working as an assistant, taking shifts according to a schedule, initially by himself and then with young doctors attached to him as assistants. Dragni had mastered the basic techniques of his medical specialty, which inspired confidence and calm in the personnel on duty. When an emergency arose, he would leave his office and quickly resolve the problems. Dragni realized quite well that he had to be a professional down to the smallest detail, to help patients and maintain his position in the clinic.

Over the years, his internal need to lie intensified. Every morning before the ward round, he would find a doctor or a nurse to start a conversation with and begin spinning tales. No one could predict what he would come up with; his stories were on par with the exploits of Baron Munchausen. He was constantly the hero in various incidents that he himself invented and came to believe in. But the personnel were used to Dragni's character, and the resident-doctors adored him. The young doctors knew of his weakness for action movies, full of gunfights and romance, and never missed an opportunity to bring him a new one for his home video collection.

One Saturday shift turned out as a decisive moment in Dragni's career, earning him the respect of all his colleagues, even his biggest scoffers. It was midday, and Dragni, still Dr. Shestakov at the time, was sitting in his office reviewing the results of the tests he had ordered during the morning rounds.

It was the middle of July, and it was unbearably hot outside. Typically, at this time of year, the capital experienced extreme heat, and this day was no exception. Dragni had opened both windows in his office, as well as the door, in an attempt to create a little coolness. His enormous body struggled to endure such a heat wave, and he was sweating and panting all over. By all appearances, the day was going to be quiet, and nothing but the heat could disturb him. He had just finished lunch and was continuing to review the examination forms when suddenly the phone on his desk rang

'Dr. Shestakov,' Dragni introduced himself, answering the phone without taking his eyes off the paperwork. The next few words he heard, however, pulled him out of his concentration, and glancing up at the bare wall in horror, he feverishly replied: 'Got it!'

He slammed down the receiver, jumped up, and rushed headlong out.

'Dimitrova!' he yelled down the corridor. 'Dimitrova!'

'What is it, Doctor?' One of the nurses on duty emerged from the nurses' station. When she saw Dr. Shestakov, drenched in sweat, flying down the corridor, her casual gaze changed to a worried expression.

'Take Grozdanska, prepare a bed in the hall! Dr. Pishmanov has been in an accident and is unconscious. They're bringing him up here any minute now.' The second nurse on duty, Grozdanska, had just appeared and heard only the last words of Dr. Shestakov, but that was enough to cause her horror and send shivers down her spine.

Dr. Pishmanov had been in a serious car accident on his way to Sofia. He was returning from his wife's home village, where they had a kind of cottage. He often liked to stop by and dig in his garden. He was one of the oldest doctors in the department and one of the people who secretly mocked Dr. Shestakov for his weakness for lies. But now Pishmanov was in critical condition, and Shestakov was the one who had to pull him out of the ditch, figuratively speaking.

The nurses on duty rushed around the intensive care unit and began their usual routine of preparing everything necessary for such a situation, when suddenly they heard a terrible commotion in the corridor and went out to see what was happening. The emergency room doctor, along with the orderly and the nurse, quickly pushed the stretcher with the patient. However, they were greatly surprised to see Dr. Shestakov running alongside the trolley as well, sweating and panting.

Once they entered the room, Shestakov assumed full control of the situation. He began giving orders and instructions on what to be done, actively participating in the procedures himself and setting an example for the others. Dr. Pishmanov's condition stabilized, and then Dragni began to look around for the traumatologists' team, which he thought should already be there to assess whether emergency surgery was necessary. The clock was ticking relentlessly for the patient, and Dr. Shestakov was becoming increasingly restless. The traumatologists were late, and he knew that every second of delay could cost Pishmanov dearly. Finally, he could not take it anymore and grabbed the phone, but just then the nurses called out:

'Dr. Shestakov, Dr. Shestakov! Dr. Pishmanov's pulse is weakening, the heart's not functioning!'

At that moment, Shestakov literally flew across the room, glanced at the monitor for a moment, and threw himself into resuscitating his colleague. He was doing the cardiac massage, but there was still no pulse.

'Grozdanska, adrenaline!' Dragni ordered in a hoarse voice. Without wasting time, the nurse injected the patient. Still, no pulse appeared on the monitor, but Shestakov did not give up. His entire body was like a soaked sponge, and Grozdanska and Dimitrova were about to burst into tears. But then a miracle happened, and the familiar heart waves appeared on the monitor. At the same moment, as if the heavens had opened up above Dr. Shestakov, he stepped back and stared intently at the monitor. Yes, indeed, the heart was working again, Pishmanov was alive!

Tears of joy were streaming down the nurses' faces. They jumped on Shestakov and hugged him with genuine, noble affection. Dr. Pishmanov, their colleague, had survived, thanks precisely to the efforts of the man he had been mocking so much. Seconds later, the traumatologists arrived and decided to perform an urgent surgery. The operation was successful, and Dr. Pishmanov survived. Yes, indeed, it took him months to recover, but he did come back to life and even returned to work.

This case literally catapulted Shestakov to the top among his colleagues, and for years afterward, they told stories of his heroism in the department.

He later became an associate professor and then a professor, so he no longer had to take shifts. As a professor, he excelled at managing the team, but he still remained a liar.

Times changed, but Dragni did not. He remained true to his life principles. One day, already retired, he had stopped by the clinic for a short visit to see his old colleagues and exchange a few words with them. Finally, before leaving, he blurted out another lie:

'Well, I'm off. Keep hale and hearty; don't give up in difficult times! Just imagine what I went through when I participated in the war in Afghanistan. I've even worked under artillery fire. Goodbye!'

He left satisfied, knowing he had done a good job once again.

PENYO THE DUCK

Penyo The Duck was a rather overweight 35-year-old man, of average height. He had wavy chestnut hair and large, slightly protruding brown eyes. His body was solid and compact, which somehow made his physique appear natural despite the extra weight.

He had married relatively young and had two daughters. His wife, however, had not been able to bear living with him and soon after giving birth to their second child, she hastened to file for divorce. Although divorce was seen as a negative phenomenon during the communist era, casting a sort of shadow over the divorcing spouses and their children, the woman nevertheless had chosen to raise her daughters alone – at the mere prospect of spending the rest of her life with The Duck, she barely hesitated to make that sacrifice.

Penyo was a city boy through and through. As a child, he loved playing with his friends, wandering aimlessly through the streets all day long, or sitting on the steps in front of his apartment building, playing cards for hours on end. At school, The Duck showed little interest in any of the subjects studied. Notwithstanding he was a truly bright kid, he had never invested more effort than necessary to just pass up to the next grade. And so, he grew up like that.

Despite the fact that our character felt most at home in the city, unlike other children he would spend his summer vacations in the village, with his grandparents, where his parents would send him every year. Following a long-standing family tradition, he was named after his grandfather, Penyo, and understandably, he was the old man's greatest weakness.

Grandpa Penyo was a master gardener. He had taken over the craft from his father, who had taken it over from his father. Thus, gardening had become a tradition in the family. The old man maintained correspondence with gardeners from all over the country, exchanging tips and advice. He knew where to get the best seeds for seedlings and was known throughout the region for his expertise in horticulture.

Although there were restrictions on free trade during the communist era, the sale of tomatoes, cucumbers, onions, garlic, lettuce, and other agricultural produce was permitted, but tightly controlled by the state in what were known as "purchase points" in villages and towns.

So, Grandpa Penyo was able to sell his fresh produce and save some money for his beloved grandson. The old man tended to his garden with great love and care. Some time ago, he had hired a specialist who had found an underground water source in his yard and had installed a water pump and so the old man had secured plenty of water for his vegetable beds throughout the summer. As a result, his garlic grew beautifully, and his tomatoes produced abundantly; pumpkins were planted in the corners of the garden, and green zucchini grew alongside them, his beds were always neat and tidy. His favorite pastime was growing cucumbers. There was nothing more delicious to Grandpa Penyo than a fine, fresh cucumber, hidden among the leaves, covered in droplets of morning dew, just waiting to be picked. Grandpa Penyo would take it, then carefully wash it and place it on the table first thing in the morning.

In addition, in his yard, the old man had chickens, ducks, turkeys, and, of course, a small pigpen with a pig that was being fattened up for Christmas. He also had a donkey named Gosho and a donkey cart, which he used to transport his agricultural produce to the purchase points in the village and surrounding district. Although Grandpa Penyo had tried over the years to teach his grandson gardening, The Duck never showed any interest in this craft. In short: he had inherited none of his grandfather's noble qualities. This however did not upset the old man too much, as the boy was, after all, his only grandson. He loved him unconditionally and always set aside the best of what grew in the family garden for him.

On the other hand, young Penyo loved to sneak into the duck houses and spend hours talking to the ducks. He would watch them sitting on their eggs and imitate their sounds, sitting on a pile of sand in the yard. The other village children would watch him from behind the hedge, giggling silently at his strange game, and eventually they had mercilessly labeled him with the nickname The Duck, which he later tried unsuccessfully to shed. Grandpa Penyo even chased away with his cane one or two of the neighborhood children who were most shamelessly insulting his grandson, but even that failed to change anything.

Quite unfortunate for Penyo, one of the village children attended the same city school and was even in his class. Thus, this unpleasant nickname was spread to the school, then to the neighborhood where he played, while, finally, the whole town began calling him The Duck. Penyo would not tolerate anyone bullying him, and several of his classmates learned that the hard way, but despite all his efforts to shake it off, the nickname persisted. Everyone knew him as The Duck, although they did not call him by that nickname to his face; instead, they simply mocked him behind his back. The nickname was so popular that even his class teacher had once almost uttered the wrong name, nearly calling him "Duck", when Penyo had broken one of the building's windows with a soccer ball.

*　*　*

With the end of communism, the nation derailed from its old path and embarked on the tracks of democracy. New political parties swarmed, agricultural cooperatives were wound up, and land was returned to its original owners by law[29]. Private property was restored, and people were free to start their own businesses according to their wishes and abilities.

During that period private universities made their debut in the educational scene. Penyo The Duck immediately enrolled in a university and, after three or four years, graduated with a degree in Slavic philology. After receiving his diploma, he tried his hand at teaching but it did not work out. He lasted two or three months before venturing into the business world, which was largely unregulated at the time.

After that brief and unsuccessful stint as a teacher, Penyo rented a stall at the market in the district town and started selling vegetables. At first, he tried to grow and sell his own produce, presuming his grandfather would do all the field work back in the village. However, the old man passed away shortly after the arrival

---

[29] In the Socialist Era in Bulgaria almost all the agricultural land (with the exception of small parcels for personal use by the people) was virtually under the full control and management of the state-controlled agricultural cooperatives or agro-industrial complexes. After the demise of Communism at the end of the 80s and the beginning of 90s those establishments ceased to exist and the land was returned to the original owners or their successors.

of democracy, and as we have already mentioned, Penyo had never bothered to learn much about gardening, even though he spent his entire childhood among cucumbers and garlic. So, for The Duck now holding a university degree, digging in the dirt and growing vegetables seemed like a pointless task.

After some contemplation, he decided it would be more profitable to buy tomatoes, cucumbers, onions, and shallots from the local villagers and sell them at the market. And he was right – the business took off, and The Duck started seeing real money.

Back then, anyone could start a company and begin buying up just about anything, from iron and paper to vegetables and woven clothes. And more importantly, purchases were supposedly made at government-fixed prices, though in most cases, the buyer determined the price on the spot, while no written traces were left of the deals. So, Penyo started buying vegetables from the village producers paying them next to nothing, then reselling the goods at double or triple the price.

Suddenly, the market stall in the district town began making money. Everyone knew The Duck because his produce was always fresh and free of nitrates – it was something buyers were very cautious about. It turned out Penyo had learned a thing or two from his grandfather after all: especially, how to pick out the fresh produce from the stale one. And his knack for quickly sensing what would sell best at the market was also apparent. *I guess spending all those summers in the village wasn't in vain,* The Duck said to himself one day. *At least Grandpa taught me how to trade. Let others plant and dig; I'll make the money,* and a smug grin spread across his face.

A few months passed, then a year, then two. The Duck gained experience at the market stall and built up his finances, and that did wonders for his confidence. Once he had saved up enough money, the first thing he did was buy a second-hand, eight-year-old Merc. This made him feel as though he had entered a higher class of people. In the neighborhood where he lived, everyone talked enviously: "The Duck has made it in life." Even his ex-wife started calling him again, and their children began to enjoy having the father they had not seen for several years.

But Penyo did not stop there; he kept expanding his business. Soon, he took on a second and then a third stall at the market. He hired people to sell for him, keeping a close eye on their work to prevent any pilfering. It was impossible to sting The Duck – he was a natural-born inspector. The business kept growing, and after a while, he bought a truck as the amount of produce for sale was increasing, and the Merc was unsuited for that kind of work.

Greed began to stir in The Duck's heart. At night, as he lay in bed, he constantly calculated in his head how much money he had made that day and how much more he could sell to become wealthy.

He had come to realize that money was what had made him to be regarded as "somebody" in the small town. He enjoyed it when people greeted him on the street, stopped to chat with him. But he was well aware that he was one of many in this line of business. There were others there and they were earning far more than he was.

As he watched all this, a plan began to form in his cunning mind. Over the next couple of months, it gradually took shape and finally crystallized into a well-conceived scheme on how to make a quick buck, or as they say: "to strike it rich".

The Duck's plan was, in essence, a carefully crafted scam, but he was not particularly worried about that. He intended to buy a large quantity of agricultural produce from farmers in several villages, promising them high prices but deferring payment until after the sale. Of course, The Duck had no intention to pay – he planned to disappear with several truckloads of prime vegetables before the farmers even realized what was going on.

It is worth mentioning here that in the early years of the transition to democracy, the market was often unable to absorb large quantities of agricultural goods, leading to tons of unsold fruits and vegetables perishing and eventually being discarded. As a result, small producers – hardworking and honest farmers – were sometimes forced to entrust their produce to buyers, whereas they would receive their share of the profits only after the goods were sold, and that share was most of the times meager. It was in this small detail that The Duck had found the key to his plan, which he intended to execute in two stages.

Having calculated every detail with mathematical precision, Penyo put his plan into action. On a hot July day, he set off with his truck to a village. As usual, he purchased and loaded up tomatoes, onions, cucumbers, and garlic, carefully weighing the produce. What was different this time, however, was that Duck paid for everything in cash. Seeing this, the villagers were overjoyed, believing they had finally encountered a decent and honest trader. Most of the producers had been cheated in the past and had become quite distrustful, so the cash in hand felt like manna from heaven. As he was leaving, the entire village had gathered to send off the honorable merchant and wish him a safe journey.

The following week, The Duck visited them again, and once more, he made a completely fair purchase of their agricultural produce, paying on the spot and in cash. It was at this point that Duck moved on to the second part of his plan. Having earned the villagers' trust, he gathered them around and spoke smoothly from the back of his truck:

'My dear fellows, as you can see, we're working well together, selling the produce and making a profit.'

'That's right,' one of the villagers chimed in. 'It's obvious – when you're doing well, we're doing well too.'

Penyo was nodding affirmatively:

'We need, however, to increase production and sales in order to further our profits. With such small quantities of the produce, we're going nowhere. We can't even buy a used car for our kids,' The Duck began to tug at the heartstrings of these hardworking people. The well-being of their children, which they equated with saving for an apartment in the city or for a used car, was the foundation of rural Bulgarian morals.

'You're right,' another villager chimed in, 'it would be good to earn more.'

They've taken the bait, The Duck thought to himself with satisfaction and continued aloud:

'I've received an offer from a Belgian company to buy a large quantity of tomatoes, cucumbers, gherkins, onions, quality peppers, and potatoes. Payment will be in francs, but it will come only after the trucks reach Belgium. I need to know if you're on board.'

There was hardly any need to ask – they were already on. Greed had filled their hearts, and the thought of francs had never crossed their minds. Some even started wondering what the exchange rate was between the lev and the Belgian franc. However, a couple of villagers became suspicious and left.

In the end, most of the villagers agreed. It was decided that the trucks would arrive in a fortnight. A well-organized plan was needed to ensure fast loading, so the trucks could head back to Belgium within two or three hours.

The Duck left the meeting absolutely satisfied. On his way home, he called three of his friends, who eagerly agreed to take part in the scam. Their job was to handcraft fake license plates with Belgian numbers for their trucks, grow beards, and learn two or three French phrases.

On the day of the event, The Duck arrived in his car in the village. When the villagers saw his Mercedes and the huge trucks with Belgian license plates, they shouted, full of joy:

'The Belgians are here, the Belgians are here!'

Everyone was anticipating big profits and had already made their plans for how they would spend their earnings.

The organization of this farce was truly admirable. The trucks pulled up, the drivers mumbled a broken "bonjour" and flung open the trailer doors. The loading was done quickly, and Penyo issued an invoice to each producer for the profit they were to receive in Belgian francs. Everyone was satisfied, each having given their best produce.

As the trucks were leaving, the villagers waved goodbye cheerfully. The trucks drove off, but not towards the border. Instead, they headed for a large produce market in a nearby city. The Duck sold everything there at a premium. Afterward, he handed out some petty cash to the "Belgian" drivers and returned home, satisfied. He had hit the once-in-a-lifetime jackpot. *Now I've really raised the bar*, The Duck thought proudly, his eyes welling up with tears. *The others will be green with envy when I buy the new Merc.*

The unfortunate farmers waited for three days in vain for their payment, their attempts to contact The Duck via phone failed. His number had been disconnected. Soon after, Penyo really bought a new Mercedes, proving his point – everyone envied him but said nothing. They knew that if he had bought a new car, it meant he was serious business now and a "big player".

Not long after that, he went to a Black Sea resort for a well-deserved vacation after his big score. But call it fate, or bad luck – to his surprise, one of the conned farmers was on the beach with his family. The farmer recognized him immediately and, without hesitation, went berserk on Penyo. A brawl ensued in front of the astonished tourists, with children screaming and crying. The police arrived almost immediately. After both men were arrested, the real reason for the fight became clear. The attacker was released, while The Duck was detained. He was eventually charged with fraud and sentenced to prison.

In prison, Penyo underwent a complete transformation, and there his nickname was changed to "The Belgian". Upon his release, he substituted the market stalls for a taxi. He started working as a taxi driver, patiently waiting for customers at the rank. The young called him The Belgian, while the older ones still called him The Duck. He never returned to gardening, and his wife and two daughters moved to the capital. They spoke on the phone a couple of times when The Duck would call to ask to see his children, but they never wanted to see him again.

ONE STRANGE DOCTOR

Night shifts in an intensive care clinic are arduous and exhausting. Since these hospital units admit patients in critical condition, it is obvious that these patients are entirely reliant on the physicians and nurses working there. A characteristic feature of a night shift in such a ward is the element of unpredictability: the incoming team never knows what challenges the night has prepared for them.

Sometimes, the work is so demanding that staff members are unable to rest until morning. And in the mornings, a doctor from the night shift will never simply leave home – he must remain until he provides an overnight report to the supervisor. While this is standard practice, the handover can sometimes be so lengthy that it becomes almost as taxing as the night shift itself. In certain moments, this can feel like a trial of one's spirit and willpower.

Dr. Petrov, a young specialist who had recently won a competitive position as a resident doctor in the intensive care unit of one of the city's renowned hospitals, worked in exactly such an environment. Despite the ward having a sufficient number of physicians, he was often left to manage night shifts alone, with just a couple of nurses and one or two orderlies.

Due to the prevailing circumstances of the time, medical students in their final year of training or even undergraduate medical students were frequently assigned to work as nurses or orderlies. This was subject to the respective hospital's human resources policies. The wages of such nurses and orderlies were low, and the work in intensive care units was rather unattractive.

In the early 1990s the collapse of communism, which was to a large extent brought about by its own inherent flaws, led to profound changes both in the society and the state administration. Naturally, the fundamental functions of hospitals remained unchanged, and their management structures persisted as well. As a young physician who had secured a position in a prestigious clinic, Dr. Petrov ended with his monthly schedule consisting of an increased number of shifts and unpaid overtime hours, particularly on weekends, of course. This "reward" was directly arranged by the clinic's chief administrative assistant.

The position of chief administrative assistant held a somewhat ambiguous status within the hospital hierarchy, as each ward had its own head and deputies. Typically, this role was assigned to a physician with many years of experience who, however, had not managed to come to be "big enough" for the rank of associate or full professor written in front of his name. While the position did not come with significant financial benefits, it offered substantial "social" advantages. This was the person responsible for preparing the shift schedules for the doctors in the hospital. He complied with his own unwritten rules only, which were tacitly accepted by all staff members. This person could arbitrarily assign shifts, always ensuring that his own name appeared first on the schedule, having chosen for himself those days that he found most convenient. Everyone sought to maintain friendly relations with the chief administrative assistant and, to the extent possible, sometimes even to appease them.

During one of his many weekend overtime shifts, Dr. Ivan Petrov met two medical students who had recently been hired as orderlies in the intensive care clinic. These friendly, clean-shaven young men were working part-time for a little extra money. They were good employees, dedicated and at the same time they both were interesting and odd characters.

Both of them were pastors belonging to some sort of alternative church. In the early days of democracy, "alternative" churches were popping up everywhere, and no one really knew how many there were or who their followers were. These two preachers had risen to leadership positions in one of these churches.

In summertime, the two pastors would open the windows in the clinic, raise their hands, and begin to pray fervently. While their actions did not seem entirely ritualistic, it was difficult to discern the extent of their performative elements. Both presented an intriguing sight to those around them as they moved among the intensive care patients with a gospel in hand or pushed into the coat's pocket. Upon finishing their shift, they would change back into their black suits, white shirts, and obligatory ties. Clean-shaven and neatly dressed, they carried expensive designer bags and seemed – something uncharacteristic for the time – cheerful, optimistic, and buoyant in their conversations.

This behavior had impressed both the clinic and the hospital administrations. In those years, the Communist Party had rebranded itself as "socialist" one, but its nomenklatura continued to hold key administrative positions in the government-related structures, including hospitals. Atheism had been the party comrades' creed for nearly fifty years. However, despite the hospital administrators' strong desire to dismiss the pastors, there was no mechanism to do so due to the inexorable democratic changes taking place throughout the country.

Subsequently, the two proved to be exemplary in their work and, moreover, managed to simultaneously carry out evangelical-education activities among the hospital personnel and patients in a most kind and humane manner. They never ceased reading the apostles' gospels and unyieldingly believed in the truthfulness of the preachings they were giving.

Eventually, to everyone's surprise, they quitted their job at the hospital quite unexpectedly, while the reason for their decision remained unclear. Despite their apparent eccentricity, they had been performing all their duties at the clinic in a perfect manner. Among the staff, there were only rumors and speculations that there had been certain disagreements with the supervisors perhaps.

In time, one of the young pastors had developed a friendship with Dr. Petrov. It might be worthy to devote a few lines here to describing The Pastor as they called him, although any such description would inevitably be incomplete. It would not be an exaggeration to say that The Pastor was a handsome young man. He had dark, slightly curly hair, neatly trimmed in a way that pleasantly and unobtrusively accentuated his strong masculine features. His face was always clean-shaven, and when one looked at him, it seemed to glow with goodness. Of average height and with an elegant physique, he was always impeccably dressed in designer suits. In addition to everything else, he had perfect manners and always smelled of fine cologne. In short, he was a charming individual. Women secretly admired him and looked up to him.

What was most striking about The Pastor was the discrepancy between his social status as an orderly, on one hand, and the clothes and accessories he wore, on the other. People wondered where this still undergraduate student, with a meager monthly salary, could find money for expensive designer clothes. To the more curious, The Pastor claimed it was only natural for him to dress in such a way, especially since his position in the church required him to maintain a certain standard. The fall of communism in the country had opened the gates for the rapid arrival of all major fashion brands to the market, and more and more brand stores opened in the capital. This, in turn, had fascinated ordinary citizens, and commerce flourished.

It could not be denied how much The Pastor cherished the sick children in the hospital. During his night shifts with Dr. Petrov, he often requested permission to go to the pediatric ward where he offered prayers filled with love and wishes for the health of those children, of the moms who were staying with their kids there, and of the attending personnel.

However, the professor of the Pediatric Clinic was a staunch atheist and could barely tolerate the presence of the young pastor. At that time, as their morals were rather questionable, professors and associate professors considered the clinics and wards in the still state-owned hospitals as their own personal domains, unilaterally dictating the rules there. About these professors and associate professors – their communist past would remain largely hidden, with only a few having their personal files disclosed, revealing their connections to the former Communist Party and the political police. Eventually, they retired, but unfortunately, there was no real change in the academic environment. The next generation of doctors, in their turn, came to power replacing the previous one, but nevertheless many of the new ones were still connected, either directly or indirectly, to the former Communist Party.

Amidst that vibrant environment, The Pastor, being a young man with a quick mind and one who had previously enjoyed many visits to various Western countries, persevered in claiming the existence of the divine providence. He spoke convincingly of God, quoting entire passages from the New Testament from memory, which truly impressed his interlocutors – usually colleagues from the Intensive Care Clinic and patients alike.

Dr. Petrov, for his part, was not quite familiar with such religious writings. In his eyes, this young, still-undergraduate medical student was the most gifted apologist for Christianity he had ever met. After all, during the communist years, access to theological literature was largely restricted. Incidentally, at the beginning of the transition to democracy, quite a few funny things had happened in the country. Former communists and the like had crossed the thresholds of the churches for the first time and began to light candles on holidays, and listen to long liturgies, which for them were like symphonies never heard before. Nevertheless, an apparent shift in attitudes towards religion was commencing.

Dr. Petrov had not undergone the rite of baptism, but through his own contemplations, he had long reached the conclusion that life *must* have its Creator. In one of his conversations with the Pastor, he asked what distinguished The Pastor's church from the local, officially recognized, Orthodox Church.

'Look, Doctor,' the young preacher chuckled, 'you are a physician and let's say, broadly speaking, you serve the patient. You care for them, you treat them, and so on. However, you have chosen your specialty, you work here in the intensive care unit, but there are other doctors as well – one works in the emergency department, another is a cardiologist and treats hearts, you get what I mean, right? Ultimately, you all are subordinate to one subject whom you serve – the patient. And it's the same case with my church and the Orthodox Church, and not only... We have some differences in doctrines and perceptions, but the common goal remains the same, and eventually we all serve God.'

The pastor was truly gifted, and whenever he preached, the church was always packed. As an undisputed orator, he had the ability to captivate his congregation from the very beginning to the very end of his sermons. He understood people's dreams, felt their desires, and possessed the magic to ignite faith and hope in their hearts.

For Dr. Petrov, it all seemed too genuine and fulfilling. He likened his friend to a true apostle. In their conversations, besides sharing his views on the world and some reflections on faith and religion, the pastor had also revealed some details of his personal life. It turned out that, in addition to being dedicated to preaching, he was also an excellent student. Petrov sincerely hoped that one day his friend would become a pediatrician and devote his knowledge and love to children.

Subsequently, The Pastor made several attempts to secure a job in the pediatric clinic of the hospital, but they all proved to be rather agonizing and futile. The professor had found The Pastor's independent spirit, his demonstrative material well-being, and his outward calmness irritating, and thus he had already been harbouring resentment towards him, to such an extent that one day he had publicly stated:

'Here, in *my clinic*, there is no place for preachers and church servants!' These words had reached The Pastor's ears, and he had bitterly realized he did not have the power to prevail over the rigid beliefs of that man or simply to please him in order to get the chance to do what he desired and where he would benefit the society at his best. With that, The Pastor's dream of becoming a pediatrician had come to an end.

Once, The Pastor picked up Dr. Petrov from work in his luxurious, newly purchased SUV. This vehicle genuinely surprised and impressed Petrov, who was getting into such a car for the first time – it made his self-esteem rising. However he was also curious about how his young friend had earned so much money to acquire a new car and a mobile phone, as these things were synonymous with substantial wealth at the time. Petrov thought it was somehow unlikely for the pastor to be some conspiratorial figure or a smuggler, for instance. As they were talking, it became clear that on New Year and other holidays, the young preacher distributed donations among the people in the church, which could range from jars of pickles and peppers to medicines and clothes. Meanwhile, he also worked as a real estate broker. In short, he made good money from numerous sources and activities.

Over the years, a spontaneous and easy friendship developed between the two. When Petrov eventually wrote his first medical book, The Pastor supported him with a small sum for its publication. On that occasion, one afternoon, he arrived at the doctor's small apartment, and with an elegant gesture pulled out a plastic bag, like those used for groceries, full of banknotes, and counted out two hundred leva. He was in high spirits and boasted that he had made an exceptional deal. He had sold a property – a half-an-acre plot of land – on the foothills of the mountain, close to the city. The buyer had been quite satisfied as both the location and the view were incredible. However, as The Pastor shared, there was a catch that the buyer was not aware of: an underground pipeline ran through the plot, making it completely unsuitable for any construction on it. And he had paid plenty of money, without the slightest suspicion of the fraud.

Dr. Petrov stared at his friend in disbelief, speechless. It was the first time he was seeing The Pastor in such a light. He tried to logically connect this present image of his friend with that of the compassionate preacher who once was tirelessly devoting all his energy to patients in the ICU and sick children in the Pediatric Clinic. Petrov failed to make that connection, but he did not return the money either.

When a person self-publishes without a publishing house, every penny is vital, the doctor thought at the time, trying to find an excuse for what he had done.

Those two hundred leva covered the money he paid to the reviewer of his book. It was an old and kind man, a retired professor, who in his turn used the money to buy a hearing aid. Subsequently, that same professor tragically died after being hit by a car on the road. As it turned out later, the accident happened because while walking he did not hear the horn of the approaching vehicle. The reason – he was not wearing his hearing aid.

Anyway, Petrov's book came into being and aroused interest among a certain circle of medical doctors.

As time passed, Dr. Petrov learned that The Pastor had complicated and painful relations with his father, who did not approve of his chosen path in life and had predicted failure, even imprisonment. All of this had led to a rift between them, which had deeply hurt the preacher. And about his father-in-law however, he would not talk at all, although a particular incident had really upset him, and he shared it with Petrov.

'What can I say, doctor?' The Pastor began. 'We had all gathered once – the family. We went to visit my wife's parents. They have an old cottage near X. We were there for the weekend with the kids so they could see their grandparents. But my father-in-law, after having a few drinks in the evening, started insulting me and making fun of my work at the church. He said all sorts of things, but I just managed to stay quiet. And then that happened – I don't know – I guess my nerves got the best of me, but things got really bad. I jumped up and hit him so hard that my wife and my mother-in-law could hardly pull us apart. And that was the end of our visit. My wife and the kids got into the car, and we drove back home.'

As claimed by The Pastor, a large part of his personal problems stemmed from his wife's character. She was deeply religious and used to give to the poor and needy everything she had been asked for. This was admirable, but lately, the situation had spiraled out of control. The gifts he brought her would quickly disappear from their home, and it was already clear that they could never achieve spiritual harmony or happiness in their household. The Pastor confessed to his friend that he was unable to alter a woman like her, but his choice of wife had been predetermined by their church community, and this was what caused all the trouble later.

Although The Pastor and his wife never got to the point of a divorce, a deep estrangement developed in their marriage. They only spoke to each other when discussing issues related to their children. However this would happen just occasionally, as The Pastor was deeply devoted to his two daughters and took care of all their needs in great detail.

Meanwhile, thousands of other problems had begun to press in on the young preacher. He had to play countless roles – from church minister to doctor and real estate broker, even document forger and many more.

At a certain point in time, his friendship with Dr. Petrov seemed to stall. Petrov continued to develop his career and was increasingly recognized as an exceptional specialist with a bright future ahead of him. His name began to be known not only among his peers but also among patients. This, in turn, earned him the envy of his colleagues, who tried in every way to downplay his qualities and achievements. Amidst all this, Dr. Petrov already had officially been baptized into the Orthodox Church.

So, months and years passed, and then one day, by chance or not, the two friends met again. Petrov did not realize it would be their last meeting. When they embraced to greet each other, he saw a gun hanging from The Pastor's waist. For some reason, this did not at all surprise Dr. Petrov. He looked his friend straight in the eye, saying nothing, but the preacher understood everything and without flinching replied:

'I'm leaving, doctor,' he said. Silence followed. 'It's no longer safe for me here, and I can't stay. Look!'

He deftly reached into the inside pocket of his jacket and pulled out a carefully folded piece of paper. He handed it to Petrov. It was not written in Bulgarian, and, back then, Dr. Petrov did not know a word of any foreign language so he asked:

'What's that?'

'A notary deed,' The Pastor replied. 'I'm moving abroad.'

At that moment, Petrov was emotionally moved, and a few tears rolled down his flushed face.

'Don't cry, my friend,' The Pastor hastened to reassure him. 'They need you in this country, but they don't need me.'

They did not speak any more; that was how they parted.

Years later, flipping through a daily newspaper, the doctor read that the authorities were searching for The Pastor for a million-dollar bank fraud. Petrov was not particularly surprised, but he was overcome with some sadness. The Pastor had never been his best friend, but he valued him and believed that people like the young preacher were capable of changing the country, as long as their energy was channeled in the right direction.

After a while, a stranger found Dr. Petrov in his clinic and told him that a friend he had not seen in a long time wanted to talk to him. And after dialing a number, he handed him his mobile phone. On the other end it was The Pastor. The doctor did not know what to say, he just listened silently to the voice on the other end of the line. His friend had gone his own way, and so was he; they were unlikely to meet ever again.

These were years of political transition and upheaval in people's morale – democracy was on the rise. One day, Dr. Ivan Petrov was taking a shift in the same clinic where he had first met his strange friend as a young man. Sitting in the same doctor's office, he contemplated everything that had happened over the years. He would not judge anyone for anything. He simply thought about the fact that somewhere in the world, there was a friend, probably on a beautiful sunny island, who could never return to his homeland. At the same time, he hoped that The Pastor had finally achieved his dream of a free life.

ABOUT THE AUTHOR

Born in 1961 in Bulgaria, I embarked on a lifelong journey driven by a profound curiosity about the human body and mind. After graduating from high school, I pursued my passion for helping people by enrolling in medical school, where I discovered my true calling—neurology. Years of dedicated practice in intensive care units not only honed my skills as a medical professional but also gave me unparalleled insight into the complexities of life, health, and resilience.

My commitment to advancing medical science led me to complete a Ph.D. and contribute to numerous scientific publications and monographs. These efforts, alongside my clinical experience, solidified my reputation as a seasoned neurologist and researcher.

Yet, medicine alone could not satisfy my need to explore the human experience. As a student, I turned to poetry as a means of expressing emotions and thoughts that science could not capture. Over the years, this creative outlet evolved into writing satirical short stories that reflect the humor and absurdity of life during Bulgaria's socialist era—a period that shaped much of my early life as a young pioneer with a red tie and later as a member of the Komsomol.

Throughout my life, I have faced challenges and celebrated successes, but I have always made space for sharing my observations and insights with others. I hope that readers of my stories will not only be entertained but also come away with a fresh perspective and a smile.

Ian Christoff

Printed in Great Britain
by Amazon